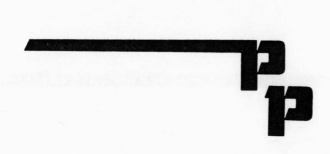

PLANET PATROL

SONYA DORMAN

COWARD, McCANN & GEOGHEGAN, INC.
NEW YORK

Library of Congress Cataloging in Publication Data

Dorman, Sonya.
  Planet patrol.
  I. Title.
PZ4.D6918Pl [PS3554.0675] 813'.5'4 78-1566
ISBN 0-698-20435-2

Printed in the United States of America

for Sherri

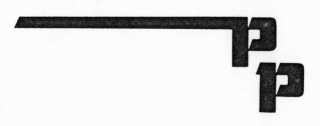

There we stood, naked as babies, lined up on the cold tile floor waiting for the doctor. Our first day at the Planet Patrol Academy. We hoped, all eight of us who were lined up, to become Planet Patrol rookies, known far and wide as Pattys for short. Plenty of prestige, and good pay. At this Academy only women in top physical condition, between the ages of eighteen and twenty-one were accepted; thirty-two was the age at which we retired from active duty, usually to get married and teach at one of the Academies, sometimes to a good job in private industry. We were from various places within the ten different Earth Dominions, and we spoke the standard British and Swahili as well as our own Dominion languages or dialects.

My friend Merle Doucette and I, both from the same area of America Dominion, had done a lot of talking about our futures before we applied to the Academy, but the only decision we'd come to was that if we made the grade we'd stay with this Interdominion police service as long as we could.

Merle was standing next to me, covered with goose pimples. A nice brunette, with glowing dark skin and one brown eye. The other eye was bright blue; she claimed that was why she was called Merle.

"Rimidon," snapped the doctor. I stepped forward. I'd grown up in a family that was serious about physical culture; my mother jogged three miles a day, and the house shook and resounded to the crash of weights my father was trying to press in the basement gym. My younger brother, Gyro, now an athlete, jogged, balanced, tumbled, and went camping with us. Self-preservation kept me in good condition.

The doctor examined me from crown to sole: five foot eight, one hundred thirty-five pounds, no scars, no moles, no difficult dental problems, vision 20/20, measured out at 36-25-38.

She said to me, "Can't you get a couple of inches off the hips? You'll look terrible in the regulation pants."

"Am I here to be admired?" I asked.

"Shut up," the Sergeant advised me. She was our house mother. A woman a lot heavier than I and not as tall. Active duty was behind her. I wondered where she had worked. No one on the staff had less than five years of active duty; most of them had much more.

Planet Patrol had evolved from Earth's old local police services out of necessity. A person in contact with home Dominion politicians, friends neighbors, and family members was less dependable in the course of duty than someone from another area or Dominion. Of course each town had its local Councilmen who'd evolved, in part, from city police. They were the new politicians who kept their own areas healthy and in order, but their powers were limited and most of them were glad to call the Patrol members for assistance. Some of the Councilmen still spoke with nostalgia of the old times when a politician had little to do but make speeches and have long lunches with colleagues, instead of going out on the street every day to talk with people, listen to their complaints, assist at accidents, and generally take part in the daily lives of their towns.

Trained troubleshooters, we Pattys would go into a central Patrol pool, and then could be called to duty anywhere, including Alpha and Vogl, the two colonized planets of our neighboring solar system.

When the doctor had finished with me, Sergeant Mother directed, "Rimidon, go to Room five for a haircut."

I got back into my clothes moodily. I knew my hair would have to go, but I should have done as Merle did, have it cut short before. You couldn't expect an Academy barber to do a decent job.

"When's lunch?" I asked.

"You just had breakfast when you got here," the doctor said. "No wonder you carry that much weight."

Merle winked at me. I tied my boot laces and went into the corridor. Plain, pale walls; overhead light behind plastic panels. Couldn't find Room 5. Rooms 4 and 6 were there, also 3 and 7. On my first day, too. Graduated third in a class of five hundred and forty; top of the judo class; long-distance runner; fluent in four languages; played cello and noseflute; but couldn't find Room 5.

While searching for it I passed a wall posted with maps. The central one was a large spread of Earth, with its ten Dominions. Three separate areas were marked with blue stars to indicate an Interdominion House of Meeting. Someday I hoped to attend a Meeting, where our social problems, advances, and retreats were discussed before the public. Any time now, they would bring to our attention the need for the colonists of the planets Alpha and Vogl to have their own Universities and Academies. The cultural and political links between them and our mother planet desperately needed to be renewed and strengthened.

I fell into a reverie in front of these maps, especially the old one from fifty years before with all those funny little jigsaw pieces indicating "national" boundaries. So many of them! I was already late for my haircut and had to move on.

Room 5 was at the corridor's end in its own little niche, with a tall glass window. I glanced outside at the grounds. They were green and pleasant, with lots of woods. I was in the central part of the building, three stories high. The dormitory wings spread out on each side, long and lower. From out there on the lawn, the Academy building looked like an expensive prep school for nice children.

"Rimidon, reporting for haircut," I said. The barber was a tall middle-aged man wearing a white jacket and the blackest Vandyke beard I ever saw.

While he was chopping off handfuls of my honey-yellow hair, I asked him, "Is this all you do all day, cut hair?"

"Don't be silly. I work with Lieutenant Kimminy in Code and Computer. I'm also married to her."

He took the clippers and bristled the back of my neck, but then he used a razor comb around the ears and front so my hair was shaped into waves and I still looked like the woman I was. "Will that do?" he asked.

"Lovely," I said. "I never would have hoped."

"Mustn't get discouraged so soon," he said.

The next two hours were spent in gym, in the swimming pool, and in bolting down a good but entirely inadequate lunch. We'd already taken the psychiatric tests and the achievement and mechanical tests, or they'd never have let us in the door.

We were lined up on hard chairs in the lounge for a briefing. The Colonel, a big blond man, reminded us that the next eight weeks were intended to test our ability to think and react quickly, our persistence in the face of difficulties, and how well we could take care of ourselves in emergencies, both physical

4

and mental. The first ten days would be spent primarily in physical training. I had a vision of a nine-foot spiked fence and a pond full of man-eating fish.

"Remember," Colonel Wayser said, just when we thought he had finished. "There is no disgrace in failing. Only half our trainees graduate into Planet Patrol. You are the cream, the elite, of young women or you wouldn't have made it this far. For those of you who do not make it, there are still excellent job opportunities at home or on a colony planet if you have a taste for frontier life."

It was largely this legend of our being the elite, the very utterly snobbish best, that caused a certain amount of hostility from people in general. If we weren't good, in fact the very best, they wouldn't call on us as they did with confidence.

We were filing out of the lounge when Colonel Wayser rumbled, "Doucette. Rimidon." Merle and I turned and faced him.

"I understand you're friends," he said. "Went to school together. It's customary here to separate friends. We feel they're likely to give each other too much support, or cover in case of mistakes."

"Yes, sir," we said.

Merle got a room on the ground floor of the west wing and I had a corner room on the second floor of the east wing. We had wondered if it would be a dormitory setup or whether we'd be locked into little cells. What we had were comfortable rooms, with a communal shower on each floor.

Since I'd been up at five in the morning to catch the plane, then the bus, I was sleepy. I took off my boots and lay down for a nap. On guard, on guard, I said to myself, as my eyes closed. Tarantulas in the wash basin? A colonel in the closet?

An ear-splitting squawk woke me. It was dark, and while I had noticed that grille above the window I hadn't really expected anything to issue from it, except perhaps a cloud of poison gas. It was squawking my name and instructing me to get down to the lounge on the double. I found my boots, put my feet into them, knocked over the lamp, picked it up, got my boots laced and my belt buckled. True enough, I didn't look so great in the blue pants that tucked into the boots. They were cut for thin women and must have been designed by some inactive person. I pulled the belt in another notch to show off my small waist and went out. The clock over the stairway informed me I'd been sleep more than two hours. I wondered if my first day at the Academy would be my last.

"Rimidon, this is Patrol," Sergeant Mother said when I entered the lounge. Besides the eight of us who'd arrived in the morning, there were half a dozen men, including the barber, who was now in regulation blue uniform. Three of the men looked tough as turnips and mean as mules.

"Yes, ma'am," I said.

"You were on call to be here six o'clock sharp."

"Yes, ma'am."

Not a smile showed on any face. Merle carefully looked at the wall. They would throw me to the fish, me and my four languages and my noseflute and my mother's hopes for me.

"Siddown," she said. There were no vacant chairs left, so I folded my legs gracefully and sat on the floor, sinking down right where I was like a lotus disappearing. One of the mules snorted.

Sergeant Mother gave the details. "At eight o'clock, you are going out on night exercises with your instructors. Doucette and Sergeant Rhodes. Blitzstein and Corporal Dale. Hardsdatter and Lieutenant Fenniman. Rimidon and Sergeant Vichek—"

The snorting mule looked over the heads at me, and I looked

6

back at him. He was tall, tough, gnarled, and gave off the brotherly warmth of an asteroid.

Merle's Sergeant Rhodes was slim and good-looking, a match for her. I wondered about Blitzstein's Corporal Dale, who seemed too young to retire to instructor. But when he moved I saw that three fingers were missing from his left hand.

Dinner was luxury foods: roast chicken, mashed potatoes, and blueberry pie, but not enough of any of them. Merle sat at the other end of the table, talking with small, blonde Selma Blitzstein. Sergeant Mother wore lipstick, which made her look a whole lot better. We had received no instructions about cosmetics and a lot of color was apparent: women's bravado, the last smear of brightness before facing the firing squad. Merle wore gold lipstick and mascara to match, and it looked great on her. I hadn't had time to apply any, but I have good skin and brown, dark-lashed eyes, so I never favor many extras.

After dinner we had half an hour in which to relax. I was surprised to see Blitzstein sitting with some kind of little tapestry frame, and I stood behind her chair to watch those thin, delicate fingers of hers work in red and gold thread, green and peacock-blue, a little at a time, slow, easy, with an exquisite patience that drew us all to watch and admire. Gradually, a bird was appearing. I'd never seen anything like that fragile work.

By eight, booted and snapped into jackets, we assembled on the darkening front lawn. A big light blazed over the front door; beyond its llumination the woods lay quiet and black. Sound of water, brook or small river, somewhere. Smell of pine trees. I could feel my senses key up.

Sergeant Vichek took my elbow sternly and turned me toward the woods. "Move!" he said.

"Would you like to tell me anything about this?" I asked, walking toward a solid wall of trees and underbrush.

7

"Roxy Rimidon," he said. I could have sworn he was grinning; the feel of it lay heavy on my back. "Keep moving."

Yes, Sergeant Mule, I said under my breath.

I'd spent some time in the woods, while growing up, and with my brother on mountain climbs. It must be on my record. None of the few forested areas left in America Dominion are completely dense; there's always a way through.

Briar bushes, I realized, betting raked across one cheek. I squinched down to get under low branches, kept my forearm raised in front of my face protectively, groped with my boots. What if I could lose the Sergeant? How well did he know these woods?

After the first thirty yards of thick underbrush, it opened out a little. The trees were larger, the small of pine stronger. I began to move out, quietly, conscious of Vichek close behind me. He dropped back a bit as I increased my speed. We did about half a mile like that. By then my eyes had good night vision, and there appeared to be something unusual about the area we were entering. The openness was all below; above, it was dense and tangled. Not right. Not nature's way of doing it. Man-made. Look out, Roxy, I warned myself, something's either going to drop out of a tree onto your head or give way under your feet.

Vichek was still audible, trampling behind me. He had big heavy feet and was lumbering along, snorting now and then. I swerved to the right and plunged into the brush. Vichek came to a halt and switched on a powerful flashbeam.

Another few feet forward and I'd have walked into a net spread on the ground and would've been hoisted into the air like a fish. I crouched, invisible, among saplings and briars. The light danced around as Vichek sought me. I stopped breathing. I practiced not being. There is a way to do it, to become leaf, twig, log.

"Rimidon," he called softly. I was motionless.

He took a few steps backward and began to search elsewhere. I breathed once. His boots made a lot of noise. Nothing like an angry mule to discourage a person. Inch by inch I moved deeper into the brush. Vichek swore noisily. He stumbled over something, recovered his balance, and asked God to send him back to active duty on Vogl. Bogs were better than rookies. By this time, I was thirty feet away from him, wondering how to get around behind him, to the path back.

Little by little I crawled through. Mosquitoes found me, and feasted. Sharp bits of bark slid down inside my shirt. I was sticky, tired, and disgusted. What kind of training is this? I wondered. Why don't they just take us for a good camping trip in the mountains? I made a couple of false starts toward the path and finally found it, though it wasn't cleared enough to be a real path. Before I stood up, I listened, but there wasn't a sound: no boots, no snorts, no Sergeant. Just the same, I stepped quietly and with great care.

Finally, I was close enough to the edge of the woods to see the blaze of light over the front door. A mule fell out of the sky and landed on top of me. I twisted over as I went down and struck upward, got a good solid punch landed. Then he had his knee in my stomach, and my arms pinned.

"Give up?" he asked.

"Ugh," I said, spitting out leaf mold. He had a terribly big, bony knee.

"Now, now," Vichek said, hauling me to my feet. "I grew up in the Sierras. You gotta admit you met your match."

"You can move quietly when you want to," I admitted.

He snorted a laugh. "Of course I can. I was afraid I was overdoing it on the way out, all the noise I made. Woman, what do you weigh?"

"None of your business," I said grumpily, scraping the bits of bark off my sweating neck. We went through the last of the woods onto the lawn and came into bright light, where Colonel

Wayser was standing. Sergeant Mother, a notebook in her hand, looked up at us. She stared at Vichek, so I turned to look and saw that one of his eyes was beginning to swell shut.

"Grade A," Vichek said, looking grim. "She's fast as a bobcat for all that weight."

It wasn't bad enough that Sergeant Vichek fell on me, but he had to remark on my weight in front of the Colonel. As if the mule didn't outweigh me by fifty pounds.

The Colonel glanced at me as I went by. I smiled at him but he only quirked the corner of his mouth a little.

Sergeant Mother said, "You're free to go to the lounge now . . . if you care to."

After I'd shaken the scraps of tree and leaf from my shirt and combed them out of my hair, I sat down in the lounge. Sergeant Vichek walked in, came over, and sat beside me. His eye was shut and turning purple. "You coulda belted me on the chin instead," he said thoughtfully.

"You didn't give me a chance to be delicate about it. After all, I didn't even know it was you, Sergeant."

"No kidding, what do you weigh?"

"One thirty-five."

"Yeah? I woulda guessed more," he replied, and chuckled as if very pleased.

Blitzstein and Corporal Dale came in and started a chess game. Vichek leafed through a magazine, until I interrupted him by saying, "I suppose you're my instructor for the whole time?"

"Ain't that our luck," he admitted, putting one hand tenderly over his blackened eye. "I'm not allowed to damage you, so you might take that into account, next time."

"Indeed I will," I promised. "I won't forget it for a minute."

He left first, and I was going when Merle, dripping wet, looked in from the doorway. "How did you do?" she asked me.

"The Sergeant won," I said. "What did you do to Rhodes? Drown him?"

"Oh, he won, too, out on the watercourse when I fell into it. If I don't get out of these wet things soon, I'll die of pneumonia. See you at breakfast, Roxy."

We were allowed a night's undisturbed sleep. Sergeant Mother had breakfast with us, then each of us was assigned to a study course. I drew Transport, of all things. I thought a duller subject would be hard to find, and went looking for Lieutenant Nelson's room gloomily. First floor, rear. She had a pleasant voice, a soft temper, and that rare plum-black skin. Her classroom walls were covered with charts: air routes and underground, snow, sand, bog, and mountain tramway. Every means of transport the planets offered were illustrated for us. She knew everything about each planet's transport system, the problems, the changes currently in progress.

Blitzstein and a thin Scandia Dominion girl, Lanni Hardsdatter, were my classmates in this course. We learned how to operate skimmers and how to trap escapees in Vogl's numbing maze of swamps and watery byways and how to cross Alpha's appalling deserts without dying on the way. Then Lieutenant Nelson took us out to a swamp on the watercourse, half a mile from the Academy buildings, and put us on Vogl bogshoes. She watched us flounder and splash. My eyes were full of mud, my knees soggy, and my muscles aching before she called it a morning. Immaculate in her blue shirt and pants, with polished boots and unmarred makeup, she escorted us back.

She said, "Rimidon, if you'd sweat off a few pounds you'd be good on those bogshoes. You have excellent balance."

"Yes ma'am, it runs in the family," I said. "My brother's a Tumbler. And do you know I can ride a horse?"

She smiled. "They don't use them, except at the resorts. Not for transport. How did you learn?"

11

"My grandmother was an equestrienne," I said proudly.

"Ah, that's one of our lost arts. So many of our animals have vanished," she said with sadness. "Nevertheless, why don't you start skipping dessert at lunch?"

And so they began to persecute me—a pound here, a pound there; lean meat and vegetables, fruit juice instead of cocoa; swim, run, jump, climb, and many an evening trying to get rid of Vichek in woods and hills. I never succeeded, though I came close a few times. I learned to respect him. Tough as he was he never pushed me too far, never lost his temper, and sometimes he even said I was doing fine.

Merle, who'd always been more ambitious and harder on herself than I, began to turn out triumphs in Code and Computer. She was the pet of Lieutenant Kimminy, who headed up that department and was married to our barber. They had a son in Patrol stationed on Alpha, and a daughter studying music in Asia Dominion. Lieutenant Kimminy wore a vague expression which disguised both a sense of humor and a genuis for cybernetics. I liked her, though I was her worst student. She, her husband, and Captain Holder worked down in the basement with their computers. One section inside the basement was walled off; a heavy metal door carried a sign which said DETONATION & DEACTIVATION. Every day Selma Blitzstein disappeared in there and reappeared only for meals or recreation. I thought of the thin, precise fingers that threaded the tapestry bird, threading the little wires and deactivating bombs. No question but that her special talent had been discovered.

"I suppose one day we'll become staff," Merle said during one of our rare chances to talk together. "I can't see that far ahead, though."

12

"Well, I wish I thought I'd be good enough for staff ten years or so from now."

"We're going to be wonderful," Merle insisted, gritting her teeth with such a determined expression that I laughed.

◆

Corporal Dale took us over to the firing range for arms instruction. I was teamed with Lanni Hardsdatter, from Scandia Dominion. Her father was a bionic engineer at one of the America Dominion neural hospitals, and according to Interdominion rights Lanni had her choice of going to her home Academy to study or staying here. She was a slim, brown-haired person with a wiry endurance that kept her going, tireless, hour after hour. Although she was not very talkative, I found her a great partner, and when something amused her she had a wonderful grin.

Several times, when we both turned out to be good shots, Corporal Dale warned us, "Don't get to feeling too big. Unfortunately, you may on some occasion have to kill a person in the line of duty. Two killings, of any kind, and you're reprocessed at a pyschiatric center right down to the last molecule, to stabilize your personalities. You want danger? You'll get plenty. People can be dangerous, and most of the time you'll be facing them with no weapon but your training."

Pattys don't carry weapons except for very special assignments. This was one of the situations where we felt the Councilmen had an advantage. They carried gas guns in case of emergency, and were rumored to be pretty free in the use of them.

When Sunday came they promised us a day off, and we had it but were not allowed to go anywhere. There had been a fire alarm—(false)—at two in the morning. We climbed down rope ladders or tumbled out first-floor windows; none of the lights worked; people yelled; Sergeant Mother called out our names and expected a response. Somewhere, two tired women had stayed in bed. This morning they went home.

Our final training test, away from the Academy grounds, was coming up. We gossiped and speculated about rumors every chance we had, but none of us really knew just what to expect.

On Thursday, at three in the afternoon, Lanni Hardsdatter and I stood in the corridor outside the Colonel's office waiting for the final assignment. Lanni whispered, "I must say, I don't feel ready yet to face the Vogl Insurrectionists."

"I don't want to face insurrectionists of any kind. Anyway, it's probably too expensive to send us to another planet before they know we can handle the job. Of course, some of the Vogl rebels may have come to Earth."

"I've heard that rumor, too," Lanni agreed. "Surely they wouldn't waste such expensive training on us and then send us out on a mission we aren't ready for?"

At this point, Merle and Selma came out of the office with grins a mile wide. I was dying of curiosity but there was no time to talk. We were next.

The Colonel gestured to a pair of green plastic chairs shaped quite unlike the back of the human form. We sat on them anyway. The colonel flipped through our dossiers, glancing from Lanni's to mine. Then, very relaxed looking, he sat back and said, "You two are going to Asia Dominion to find a dog."

It was impossible to look him in the face, but when Lanni and I looked at each other, neither of us could keep from laughing.

The Colonel said, "It's not a joke. There is a very valuable dog missing. I've been assured it is not lost. It is either injured and unable to get home on its own, or it has been stolen. The dog's owner was hurt trying to find it and has requested Patrol

14

assistance. Please go and locate the animal." With that, he closed both dossiers, dropped them into a desk drawer, and turned his attention to other papers.

Unbelieving, Lanni and I rose and slunk out. When the door closed, Lanni gave several grunts of shattered laughter. I said, "It's not that I don't like dogs, but it certainly doesn't sound like a very daring last assignment for us."

We avoided the lounge, where the other rookies were animatedly discussing their travel plans. I went to pack. And when Sergeant Mother came in she found me sitting on the edge of my bed in a pile of half-folded clothes. I wasn't doing anything.

"Brooding?" she inquired. "Don't you like your job?"

"I haven't really started my job," I mumbled.

"Don't sit there feeling sorry for yourself, whatever else you do, Roxy. You did get a final assignment, didn't you? You do understand the job needs to be done?"

"Yes, ma'am," I groaned.

"Then what's wrong with you?"

"How am I going to go out there and tell the others I'm being sent to rescue a dog?"

"Tell them anything you please, but get going. How do you know it won't be the greatest adventure you've ever had?"

She was right. I was supposing in advance that it would be nothing but humiliation all the way through. As a matter of fact, Asia Dominion was one of the few parts of our world where any real wilderness was left. There the encroachment of domed cities with their enclosing circles of industry had been checked, years before, in order to save the last few free, primitive areas. Perhaps we could have saved more if the two colony planets had been settled earlier—Vogl to farm and feed us back home, and Alpha to supply us with minerals and fuels.

Sergeant Mother went on, "Your travel orders are

15

downstairs at the door and your bus leaves in twenty minutes. It's been a pleasure knowing you, Roxy, and I look forward to hearing about you in the future."

"Thank you, ma'am," I said, and began squashing my clothes into the suitcase. I certainly didn't want to miss that bus, and if I knew Lanni she was already seated in it.

The bus took us to the rocket port, where we had time for a snack of cold juice with some crackers of the kind we used to joke about at school. They were a peculiar color due to the soy-flour base but had a good, nutty crunch in your mouth. We were still brushing off crumbs when our flight was called.

Rocket travel isn't exactly local; it takes too long to get up and level out. But for thirty years it's been the answer, for those who can afford it, to long-distance travel. It's also rather soothing, as we found out on this first flight of ours. By the time we'd both read the assignment fax sheet on the dog, the owner, and the area, we'd fallen asleep leaning on each other. It wasn't until deceleration that we woke. We were on the way down through clear skies to the coastal port of Akita.

Lanni looked at the bright white ground floating up toward us and said reflectively, "They promised us snow gear. I hope they didn't forget."

They didn't forget. When we tracked down our helicar pilot we found him leaning restfully against his machine with our equipment, including boots, parkas, and backpacks, in two nylon bags lumped at his feet.

"In you go," he said cheerfully, pushing us into the plastic bubble-belly of the helicar. It was cramped, but more flexible than a helicopter and it could traverse a variety of terrains on its wheels—but not, the pilot smilingly assured us, the kind of ice and snow we were about to encounter.

Lanni hugged herself and chattered, "Brr."

16

It looked like an angry bear, but I was in no position to observe it at leisure while it growled and came toward me slowly.

"Don't move," Lanni said under her breath. "I think that's the Akita inu, dog of Akita." She breathed audibly, once. "Or is it?" she asked.

It took all my discipline to stand where I was, boots planted in the snow, while the massive animal advanced. It had silver markings around the eyes. Its muzzle, broader than a bear's, was black. It continued to advance with great dignity, in no hurry at all. After the first growl, the animal made no other sound.

Behind it there was an open, snowy field, at the bottom of which stood a group of evergreens, like a clump of parachutes. Set in the midst of these was the hunting lodge. A man in heavy winter clothing limped out of the lodge and shouted a command to the animal. It stopped moving forward. The man walked up toward us, across the open field. When he was near,

17

the animal pivoted on its hind legs to keep itself between us and its master.

"Patrol," the man stated, looking at us with no expression on his face. I was still keeping my eye on the animal, and although it appeared not to notice me anymore, I was sure that if I made a sudden move it would be my last move. I couldn't imagine the time, now long gone, when many people had animals like that around the house. They must eat enough for two people, I thought.

"Roxy Rimidon and Lanni Hardsdatter," Lanni said, introducing us.

"Mr. Makara," he said, accepting our introductions. We moved carefully toward him. The animal backed down without giving the impression that we had anything to do with his motion.

"Yoji'nbo, one of my dogs," Mr. Makara said, putting his hand on the animal's head. "He's an Akita inu, dog of Akita."

Agile as a cat, despite his size, the dog swung around and preceded us to the lodge. We passed a shed where hunting gear was stored: sleds, packs, foam quilts, and other items I didn't recognize. The Preserve, one of the few of its kind left, was stocked with big game which had vanished from other areas. Rich people came from every Dominion to hunt animals they had only known before in their dreams. It was an expensive and privileged activity, and the limit on animals taken very carefully counted and planned in advance. In a year of bad weather or other trouble, the Preserve could be closed until the correct number of animals was reestablished.

Mr. Makara slid open the lodge door. Before we entered, I turned to look at the mountainous landscape. Empty, half-frozen, archaic; a thousand square miles of Hunting Preserve on a big coastal island in Asia Dominion; something out of past times, out of our history. To the north rose the mountain Ganju-san, six thousand feet high.

Mr. Makara was quite lame and carried one arm in a sling, and I realized the blank expression on his face must come from his efforts to hide any signs of pain. While he was out hunting for the lost dog a storm had come up, and he had taken a bad fall.

Mrs. Makara came to greet us, carrying a tray of hot soup and small plates of food. Her husband said, "We have not had the honor to welcome Planet Patrol in the Preserve before today."

"We don't have any rank yet," I explained. "We aren't officially Pattys yet."

Mrs. Makara began to chat with me. Her manner was shy, but she bored right in, finding out about me with a cheerful curiosity that I liked. "Where are you from?" she asked. "What part of America Dominion?"

"A city called Savannah," I told her, and fell into the soft dialect of my childhood, which I thought would entertain her.

She smiled. "I have never heard that before," she said. She was a pretty woman, and even in the bulky winter clothing she looked slim and strong. I sensed a sharpness, like a good steel edge, within her.

After we'd eaten, and drunk the bowls of hot soup, Mr. Makara suggested we leave the lodge, which was the ancestral home of many generations of Makaras, and go out to look at his kennel.

We followed him through a path shoveled out of the snow-banks to the rear of the lodge. Akita inu, like other breeds of dog, was rare. None of these animals had been exported to either Vogl or Alpha, the freight space being too valuable for anything but food stock.

Mr. Makara swung me in through a steel gate he had opened. We were assulted by a wave of scrambling dogs that rose on their hind legs to lick our ears, breathe into our faces, and greet us. "These are the young ones," Mr. Makara said, and showed his amusement at my surprise.

A lion-colored pup with a black face put her paws on my shoulders and snorted delicately at me, then dropped down and danced away, her golden tail plumed up over her back in the curl typical of all northern dogs. After the first wave of investigations they quieted down, so we could admire them without being overwhelmed.

Mr. Makara explained, "It was the sire of this litter that vanished. These dogs do not get lost, they track very well. We believe he came to harm somewhere. Six days ago he was sent with a hunting party. They were careless." Mr. Makara's lips turned down with displeasure. "They returned to the lodge without him and couldn't even remember when they last saw him. I went with Yoji'nbo to look for him, but much new snow had fallen and even he could not pick up the trace."

I looked over the restlessly moving group, at the diversity of coat color, and asked, "What color was the dog?"

"A sesame, like Yoji'nbo, silver underneath, dark on the outer coat. He has a white front stocking, and a white 'flying crane' mark on his chest." He looked me full in the face with the same curiosity his wife had turned on me. "His name is Tettsui. He is my best dog. Alone, he can hold a grown bear for the hunter. How are you, two young women who have never had dogs, going to be able to find him?"

I looked back at him. "We'll find him, sir. If he's still alive, we'll bring him home to you."

"Good. Let's go look at a map of the Preserve."

Lanni was much better at details than I, and had a better memory. She bent over the map with Mr. Makara, memorizing his advice as he gave it, making a few notes. Meanwhile, Mrs. Makara showed me the room where we would stay overnight.

She said shyly, "I don't know what to call you."

"Call me Roxy, we have no rank yet."

"And if you do well? You will have a good rank?"

"We will be members of Planet Patrol. Most people call us

Pattys. To get a promotion, I have to keep on doing well, and make very few mistakes."

"Ah," she said. "I did not know. We are very isolated, living here. It is part of our job, as guides and keepers of the Preserve. All we see are hunters who come and go, and sometimes one of our Councilmen. We asked them for help, but they were busy in Sakata overseeing because of the annual Theater Exhibition. A live dog—if he is still alive—can't wait." She sighed. "A cousin I have not seen for many years is a Patty, too. He went to an Academy in Soviet Dominion, the one in Snezhnogorsk."

It was my turn to say "Ah!" Snezhnogorsk was one of the first dome cities ever built in the polar north. Night lasted for months there and the temperature could drop to eighty below freezing. During the last forty years, it endured and expanded so successfully it was used as the model for dome cities on the planet Alpha, where in the desert fringes the temperature rose from below frost to intolerable heat within twenty-three hours. It occurred to me that I shouldn't feel bad about this job, considering how many parts of Earth I still hadn't seen, smelled, touched, or tasted. If I couldn't get to Snezhnogorsk, I might, one day, get to Interdominion North, where the big meetings of Dominion presidents were often held in a similar dome city.

We planned to go out at dawn to search the pass where the last hunting party had camped. The dog, Tettsui, if still alive, must be in that area. Lanni and I excused ourselves early and went to bed, but we lay awake talking for a while, to comfort ourselves for being such raw recruits faced with such a puzzling job.

I asked Lanni, "When this is over, what are you going to do during leave before our first real job?"

"I want to visit my father. He's a bionic engineer and has been working on cyborgs."

"You mean those half-animal, half-electronic concoctions?"

In a pained voice, Lanni protested, "They aren't concoctions. What do you think the old pacemaker, the artificial heart, is but an electronic part of a mammalian body?"

"I know about those, all right. But isn't a cyborg more like a metal construction with human parts? I don't see any use for such things."

"Believe me, if the technique can be perfected there are plenty of applications. My father's devoted most of his life to that kind of work. But the public feels the way you do about it, I'm afraid. Still, it isn't that different from an orthopedic surgeon. Your mother puts plastic bones into damaged people."

"Lanni, there's a world of difference! But sure, the electronic heart-lung system has saved many lives, so of course it's worthwhile."

"Are you going to visit your mother?"

"I'd like to. She travels so much, though, I don't know if she'll be home. My brother Gyro's in training for the next Games."

"Oh, yes, the Tumbler," Lanni said, as if being an athlete were beyond her imagination.

After a while, we fell asleep in the dark. It was dawn when we woke up. A litter of newly weaned pups was penned in the kitchen wing and I took time to watch Mrs. Makara feed them. The pups plunged into the pan of food, trampled through it, and knocked each other over. Their ears weren't up yet and hung into the food. When the pups were full, they sat down and cleaned each other off.

"It is a nice litter," Mrs. Makara said. "I enjoy them."

"Do you do all the care of the dogs?" I asked.

"Yes, Roxy. It is my life," she said. "Mr. Makara does the training for the hunt. That is his life." She glanced north and smiled. The reflected gold of sunrise struck against the magnificent height of Ganju-san. "I am from Katmandu. The mountains have always been my home." She gave me that shy, curious look. "And you are from Savannah. Do you have parents there?"

"My mother's there. My father was a sea farmer until he was killed in an accident several years ago."

"Was it a surface farm, like the one in Akita?"

"No, continental shelf. My mother's family runs it now. My brother could have worked it but chose something else."

"It was a disappointment to your mother, then?"

I could have told her no, my mother was content, and I was proud of my brother, but Lanni came in asking if I was ready to go.

We started west, toward the Pass of the Anvil, named for its danger as well as its shape. Yoji'nbo and Mr. Makara went ahead, but never out of sight. Although Mr. Makara had little to say to us and did not seem very responsive, I could see and even envy the bond of affectionate respect between him and Yoji'nbo. I thought if he felt the same way about the missing dog, Tettsui, the loss was greater than Patrol could understand.

Mr. Makara's limp became more pronounced and we could see he was tiring. He'd insisted on starting us out in the right direction, obviously without any confidence in our ability to find the way. I trusted Lanni, with her gift for map reading and her understanding of topography.

When Mr. Makara stopped on the trail, Yoji'nbo, too, stopped, but he sniffed the wind as if he would've liked nothing better than to go on.

"I will leave you here," Mr. Makara said. He pointed with his chin at a mass of high rock, swept clean of snow by the wind, in the near distance. "From there, you will find your way."

We adjusted our backpacks and went on. By noon we had made it up through the Pass and had a view of coastal plains in the far blue distance. We ate a cold lunch of tuna baked in kelp, spicy and good, which Mrs. Makara had packed for us. Then we went on, swinging northward according to the map, so that Ganju-san was again in view, just the peak, on the other side of the Pass.

It was wonderful country, though rough going. My early camping had been in green mountain parks, nothing so rocky and difficult. We'd had small animals—fox, varying hare, weasel, some serpents, and in the lowlands, rabbit and wood-chuck, though few of them remained now. In this wilderness of bear, wild boar, deer, and ice-capped mountains, I felt a sense of time stretching far behind me, as if I could remember the old days when the planet teemed with wildlife and clean rivers.

Lanni unfolded the map and pointed to a mark, "They camped here, under some evergreens," She looked into the distance, squinting. Evergreens abounded. We must be somewhere close by now. I started to say so and she gave me that rare, lovely grin of hers and said, "You talk. I find," and went off ahead of me.

It wasn't that hard, after all. Mr. Makara had marked the way accurately. The camp had been in a group of needle-leaved evergreens, near a partially frozen brook. The campfire had been built in the open on the brook's bank; we could use the same place if we wanted a fire. My shoulders were sore from the unaccustomed weight of the heavy pack, and I was glad to get rid of it and busy myself with putting up our freeziplastic frame. Tonight, when we rolled into our foam quilts, the clearance of the frame would be about six inches above our noses. Not roomy, but it would conserve body heat and keep off rain or snow.

"I doubt the dog's still alive," Lanni said. "Five days with no food . . ."

"But Mr. Makara said he would be if he had water, or snow to eat."

"Well, I don't see it," she grumbled. I knew by now this was her way of thinking out loud, selecting and rejecting leads to follow. Our packs contained canine medication as well as food for the dog—if we found him alive.

I prepared our supper while Lanni laid the map out flat and squatted beside it, mumbling, running her finger over the different areas. She was a bit like a good hunting dog herself. "He said," Lanni began, then stopped and put her finger on another place, "here, maybe. He said there were old rock slides, holes, caves, broken places. He said maybe Tettsui went in, got caught by the collar, and couldn't get free." She looked up as I brought the container of self-heating rations to her.

"Thanks, Roxy. Did you know they use nylon collars on these dogs? If they're caught, they can chew themselves loose."

"No, I didn't. That's barley stew there, Lanni. It's nice and hot."

Absentmindedly, she put her finger into the stew, licked her finger, put the container down, and stared again at the map. None of that dedication for me—I sat down and ate. But I did say, "Then he can't be hung up by the collar, or he would have chewed it off."

"Only if he could reach it." She suddenly got down on all fours and twisted one arm up in back, as if pulling a collar up from the back of her neck. "Like this," she said. "Even if my face, my muzzle I mean, was as long as a dog's, I couldn't quite reach it, could I?"

She looked so comical there it was hard not to laugh at her. Suddenly it began to snow—fat, slow flakes drifting down lazily in the darkness. "That's just what we need," I complained. "Complete obliteration of all tracks."

Lanni sat down and began to eat ravenously, as if she'd just discovered the food. We were so different, it was funny we worked well together. Perhaps the differences balanced. No

25

doubt the Academy knew all about us and thought we'd make a good team.

"Tracks are long gone," Lanni said.

"I know. I wasn't going to look for any. We have to find the kind of place a dog would hole up in if he were injured, or got caught. Maybe the ground caved in somewhere."

"I, personally, am going to sleep," Lanni announced. "Almost immediately, and for the whole night."

That was another difference between us. The tougher the job or contest, the more relaxed and calm Lanni appeared, while I work better if I'm keyed up to meet the pressure. Yes, sir, they know us, all right. It wasn't just luck that teamed us.

We were cold by the time we crawled into the freeziplastic, making a kind of bundle of our quilts around the two of us, sharing our body warmth to keep comfortable. We drifted off to sleep, two tiny pieces of toast in the wilderness. My last waking thought was how fortunate we were that bears hibernate in this weather and don't come visiting.

It was just getting light when Lanni breathed in my ear, "Did you hear that?"

"No, what is it?" As soon as I spoke, I heard twigs crackle. My breath hung visible just above my face, and though we'd slept in our winter caps, my head felt as cold as stone. The air was bitter. "Maybe just frost?" I asked hopefully.

My question was answered by a raucus screech, at which we both jumped up, knocking aside the freeziplastic shelter with its light coating of new snow. The bird, with its stained glass–blue body, flew over, screeching again.

With an unusually dramatic gesture, Lanni clutched her head and said, "I've got to get over being scared by everything."

"I don't see why, Lanni. Can't we just go ahead, be scared, and try to find the dog anyway?"

She glared at me. "Why do you always sound so sensible?" Before I could answer that, she yelled, "I'm freezing! Let's get going."

We ate our breakfast standing, or rather dancing and stamping around in our boots. We pretended it was to keep warm, but it was more for the pleasure of making noise and the chance it would scare off anything unexpected, and possibly horrible, that might be lurking. During the final part of our performance, while we were stamping and chewing at the same time, the sun burst up from the cold white horizon and everything around us turned gold. Lengthy shadows of blue and violet rushed across the humped surfaces. We were suddenly fifteen feet tall on the snow, and for a moment we flung our arms around and made grotesque shadow-shapes just for the fun of it. Then we shrugged into our packs.

"Over there," I said, pointing to the distance where a jumble of rock showed blue and frozen gray through holes in the snow blanket. "Might be a cave over there."

If there were any caves, they were stuffed with snow. The rocks lay in a mass, some of them broken, with sharp edges showing. Most of them must have lain in that formation a long time because lichen was growing on them, and they were ancient and weathered. Nothing was trapped or hidden there but silence.

I said, "If the dog was hunting, he may have been in the open but he may also have been under cover. There doesn't seem any way to tell."

We looked away across the country to the forest, the green arms of balsam and black pine carrying white burdens, their tops ruddy with sunshine. We put our heads down to watch our footing and trudged on. Every time we glanced ahead, the changing light had changed the scene—there was less gold, more dazzle. We stopped to put on sunglasses. We'd been warned about snow blindness. Then everything looked smoky and untrue, as if bewitched.

We pushed through new snow up long, sloping passages toward the forest. Razors of wind, in sharp gusts, cut away the snow edges and made our faces smart. All the uphill work through the drifts caused our leg muscles to ache and cramp. We had to stop now and then. To our right, northward, ran a long rocky ridge where the snow was smoking off the crests and making a strange howling sound that fell silent when the wind died, then rose again, keening and whistling.

"That's really very odd," Lanni said.

"It certainly is," I agreed. "I've never heard anything like it. Well, wait a moment . . . yes, I have. But it sounds crazy. Once in a city on a very windy day, I heard that same sound as the wind came down the streets from up around very tall buildings."

"But there's nothing like that over there," Lanni pointed out. "Come on. We ought to get under the trees before we stop to eat. And we aren't sure we're going the right way."

"The hunting party told Mr. Makara they'd worked northward, after deer, and had been in a forest. It has to be the right way," I said.

Lanni started off ahead of me just as another gust of wind came from that northerly direction, and again I heard the strange whistling howl from the ridge where the snow was almost gone, exposing broken granite faces like the ruins of an old city.

"Come on!" Lanni yelled.

"No," I shouted. "Come back!"

She didn't come back, but stopped, waiting for me to catch up. I shook my head at her and turning, tramped up toward the ridge.

"Roxyyy," she called. The sound of my name was snatched off by the rising wind and blown away to the south.

Without turning my head, I gestured with one arm and hoped she would follow. We were both fairly stubborn, so I thought it best to keep going and look as if I were not going to wait for her. I hoped we wouldn't get separated. It would be stupid and dangerous in this kind of country. Snow granules were making my eyes water and stinging my face as I headed into the wind. It moaned and cried along the ridge and I could feel the hairs on my neck standing up in response. A dog does that, I thought. A dog hears a strange sound, and its hairs rise up, and with all my intelligence and training and ambition, I am not one bit different! It seemed marvelous to me, in a funny way, though I don't know why. It was as if I retained some important sense that was almost lost to my world, as if I were proof of something good about my species.

As I neared the ridge I had to slow down for steeper and rougher places. When I glanced back once, Lanni, in the distance, was following. I could tell by the angle of her shoulders and the set of her chin that she was disgusted with me. I knew I might have to apologize for taking us far out of our way.

Ice was forming along the edges of snow where rock thrust through. Fortunately, there wasn't too much of it yet. Some of the rock was loose. I almost fell several times and had to go painfully slowly. The eerie whistling seemed to come from different directions, so that I was constantly fooled about which way to go. After a while, only my stubbornness kept me going at all. I dreamed of hot soup, warm feet, and sandy southern beaches.

Almost to the top of the ridge I stopped. Turning like a weather vane, I tried to place the sound, to pin it down. Below, to the west, snow, ice, and rock lay in chaotic piles. When I shifted my position, I could see what looked like caves, dark openings in the random mass of mountain. Wind whistled through these. Was I really going to crawl into one of them? Was there no other way to do it?

I sat down. I'd wait for Lanni. We'd consult.

The consultation consisted of Lanni looking where I pointed, listening while I said we ought to look into it, and her answer, "You bet!"

Down we went, sliding, stumbling, our packs shifting on our backs, the wind pushing us along. The pitch of the whistling seemed to rise as we approached; our ears sang with it. The first dark opening wasn't a cave, just a hollow among broken rock where snow hadn't fallen and another opening like a chimney at the top. It was here the wind rushed through and made its flute music. There were other such places. We went from one to the next and to the next, increasingly downcast at the barrenness of the place. Nothing lived here. How could a dog survive?

I insisted we turn back and go on to the top of the ridge. Down the north slope, still in heavy blue shadow and thick with old snows, lay other areas of jumble and ruin.

"As long as we're here, we've got to look at them all," I said.

"How about some soup? Or mint tea?" Lanni asked.

I shook my head. "We'll need it more later," I replied, though I never wanted anything so much as a hot drink, right there and then. "Believe me, Lanni, when I get time off, I'm going to a warm place and bask like a lizard."

"Ha," Lanni said, "you know what'll happen? They'll send you to Scandia Dominion, up on the Arctic Sea someplace near my home."

We smiled at each other, keeping our spirits up. I tightened the waist strap of my pack a little, so it wouldn't shift on the scramble down over loose rock and ice, and took the lead.

There were hollows, some clean of snow, some choked or half full, with ice forming at the edges. In one place, where yesterday's sun must have struck, snow had melted and re-

30

frozen in a fringe of icicles that now hummed and vibrated in the rushing cold air. It was desolate, confusing, spooky terrain, and the more I thought of crawling into a cave somewhere, the less I wanted to do it.

Lanni suddenly grabbed my arm. We both heard it. A change in the wind's song? Some loose stone tumbling down a frozen slope? I started to criss-cross through the area, trying to locate a specific place where the sounds came from. There was one cave, which I crawled part way into on all fours, praying there was no brown furry bear asleep in there. Not so much as a bone or a straw, just a cover of snow on the ground which hid sharp edges I had to crawl over. My knees were bruised right through the heavy pants. Lanni helped me crawl out, backwards, by pulling and guiding my ankles. There wasn't room to even turn my head and look.

"I don't want to do that again," I said when I stood beside her.

Undecided, we stayed there a few minutes. Clouds were forming high up, far away, thin and shredded in the pouring winds. On the surface of the ridge above us, the sun still dazzled, throwing weird shadows down toward us like an army of monsters. Now and then the wind fell away, giving us a few moments of quiet. During one of these lulls, a sudden long drawn howl sounded. It was farther down the north slope, toward the foot of the ridge. We couldn't see any caves there at all, though there were many boulders lying around.

"That's a dog?" Lanni asked.

"That's got to be a dog," I said. "They don't have any wolves here.

"Maybe it's something we don't understand," Lanni suggested as we slowly skidded and slipped down toward it.

The howl came again, rising in uneven little jumps of sound, only to trail off on a high note as if the wind had blown it away. Suddenly, the howl was followed by a whole series of short yips.

"Tettsui," Lanni cried, and I yelled, "We're coming, dog, we're on the way."

We bumped into each other and nearly fell as we scrambled out of loose rock to hard ground, heading for one of the boulder piles. It occurred to me that maybe something other than a dog made sounds like that, although I had heard dog sounds often enough in animal recordings, and just yesterday I had listened to the young ones yap and howl at the Makara kennel when the food was brought out.

No sooner had we reached the jumble of stones than the howl sounded from somewhere else, farther down the slope. There was twisted scrub growth down there, but I couldn't imagine it hiding a large animal. The dog's voice, if that's what it was, sounded fainter and weaker, as if the first great outcry had taken all its remaining strength.

Lanni pounded down ahead of me and bent into the scrub tangle. I was soon beside her looking at rock that was covered with lichen and snow and a crevice, or mouth, in the ground itself. The crevice was more than two feet wide and flared out below the surface into gloom, from which a snuffling and whimpering came. We could see a dog in there, perhaps eight or ten feet below us, but it was hard to make him out for there was snow in there, fallen rock, and darkness.

I put my face down to the opening. "Tettsui," I called, trying to pronounce it as Mr. Makara did.

His voice came straight up at me: "*Yarr, yarr, yarr,*" gurgling as if with happiness, accompanied by snuffles and snorts, as if he couldn't contain himself. But the sounds were not very strong, and in a minute there was silence, as if he had lain down to die after this last contact with people.

Lanni already had the nylon climbing line unsnapped from her backpack. When I was attached to one end of the line, Lannie wrapped the other end around one of the boulders, for safety back-up, and then took up the slack around her waist, holding it with both hands, in the Academy-approved fashion. There was no question or discussion about who was going down there to get the dog. I squatted down and looked again into the crevice. It I tried to jump, I might land on the dog and finish him off, or fall into some unseen deeper hole and finish myself off.

Putting both feet into the opening, I slid backward and downward, as if I had a ladder to step on, holding onto the edge first with my forearms, then with my hands, so that Lanni wouldn't have to hold my weight longer than necessary.

At least, I thought, the dog's had snow for liquid, and I have food for him in my pack. I didn't want to think about how I'd handle it if Tettsui were severely injured. Mr. Makara hadn't said a word about that possibility. Maybe he assumed I'd know what to do.

I was dangling free, trying to get my feet straight under me for the drop, as Lanni played out the line and lowered me inch by bumpy inch into the pit. Suddenly I could feel hard-packed snow under my feet. I staggered off balance before I stood, trying to adjust to the gloom. The dog was standing. I could just make out the way his tail wagged a very little bit, plumed up over his back, pale silver in the gloom. I thought bitterly that he didn't welcome me much. But I was wrong.

As soon as I said his name aloud, he took a rather feeble lunge toward me. It was so unexpected I went right down on my rump. Tettsui lay across my legs snuffling and licking my face, making sure I was a friend before he trusted himself to me.

Lanni peered down at us and I waved, which was difficult with the dog on my legs and my pack slung round in front of me. "He's alive," I shouted up.

I rummaged in my pack. Mrs. Makara had put in a dozen hard-baked biscuits of the kind used to feed dogs on hunting trips. I was afraid Tettsui would take my hand off when he smelled them, but he lifted a biscuit most delicately from my grip. Lying right there across my knees, pinning me to the ground, he held the biscuit upright between his front paws and crunched. My stomach rumbled. I thought of hot lentil soup. Even of roast chicken. Ice cream. Angel cake. Spiced tuna patties. As fast as Tettsui finished off one biscuit, I handed him another. He never moved off my legs; he just lay there going *chomp, crunch, mumpf,* as if he were at a banquet. It did my heart good to see him munch and swallow.

Tettsui licked his nose. I put my hand out carefully and patted his head. "Good dog," I said.

What a mistake! He leaped up, knocked me flat, and sat on my stomach and washed my face. Oh joy! The happiness! The full stomach after days of starving! I guess I made sounds like *glug* and *mumblf,* because Lanni called down to me.

"Are you all right?" she wanted to know.

"You oaf," I said to the dog. "You awful big ox, I have to get us out of here."

He seemed to understand because he got off my stomach and allowed me to stand up. He stood patiently, with just a slight wagging of his tail, while I made a rope sling for him, as if he were saying to me, "Good person."

"Lanni? Time to pull, but please go slow . . . I don't know how he'll take it."

He gave a little yipe of surprise as his weight shifted in response to Lanni's upward haul. "Hold on," I said, putting my arms under his chest and lifting. He yiped again as his four feet rose from the ground and began to struggle. "Hold on, Tettsui," I said, as soothingly as I could. "Good boy. Good dog, take it easy. Easy does it." So I talked him up out of reach of my hands, but I didn't know how Lanni was going to be able to get him up over the lip of the frozen ground.

I should have given Tettsui more credit. No sooner was his head free and in the air than he put both front paws on the ground right in front of Lanni and scrambled up. Snow, ice, and dirt rained down on me as I jumped out of the way. I saw his hind end disappear and heard a surprised cry from Lanni.

"Okay?" I called up. "Is he all right?"

There was a moment of nothing. Then Lanni, in an astonished voice, said, "He's sort of *dancing*," as if she couldn't believe her eyes. Looking up, I saw something whip past overhead, as if the dog had jumped across the crevice opening.

Lanni undid the sling knots and lowered the line for me. She looked down into the pit. Right beside her was Tettsui's dark muzzle pointing down, too.

"Do you want me to jump for it?" I asked.

"Oh, good heavens, no," she cried. "You'll pull me right down with you. Why didn't you stay on that diet? I know you weigh a ton. How am I going to get you up?"

"Pull," I yelled, feeling out of sorts by this time, hungry, bruised, tired. The excitement of success had worn off.

"*Yarr*," Tettsui said helpfully.

The first time Lanni hauled I only made it a few inches off the ground. The next time she gave a warning shout, and I sort of picked myself up in a half-jump, and at the same time Lanni gave a tremendous pull, so I got my fingers on the broken edges of the opening. It was only a couple of feet above me or I wouldn't have made it. While Lanni helped me climb up over the edge, the dog put his nose between us, making small, encouraging sounds. At one point, he stuck his nose into Lanni's ear, and as she shrieked, "Stop it!" I almost fell back into the pit.

Finally we sat in the midst of unstrapped packs and snarled nylon line, and popped the rims from the self-heating containers of soup, three of them. We held out on Tettsui's until it had cooled, for fear he would burn his mouth. We watched as he got his tongue neatly into a container never intended for a dog's convenience and slurped out the soup with as much relish as any Patrol member on field duty. There was a long, bad slash on his left front leg, crusted over with dried blood and dirt, but we thought it best to get him back to the kennel before trying to clean the wound.

At first, we foolishly let him set the pace, and an hour later found ourselves gasping for breath. Lanni said, "I know this breed of dog is supposed to be hardy, but he is something special. If I'd been on nothing but ice water for five days, I'd never go home so fast."

He did tire, though, long before the lodge was in sight. Tail uncurled, head down, he plodded wearily at our heels. When at last we came in sight of the lodge, Tettsui had just enough spirit left to raise his head and sniff the wind in the growing dark. There were howls and barks from the kennel; his mates knew he was coming home.

Mr. Makara came out with a lantern. "Oh, Pattys," he exclaimed, "you have found him!" Tettsui lay at Mr. Makara's feet, rolled over on his back with his paws in the air, and made little howls and cries of hello. Lanni and I reeled into the lodge, where Mrs. Makara put her arms around us both.

"We are so grateful," she said. "We never thought you could find him. Are you hungry?"

"Ravenous," I said, helping Lanni with her pack. We shucked out of packs and parkas right there, too tired and overwhelmed to be polite or careful. Mrs. Makara couldn't have cared less. She disappeared into the kitchen, and by the time Mr. Makara came back from the kennel she had given us one of her trays full of steaming, spicy food. I could have howled with pleasure myself, but settled for a smile.

"The cut has almost healed," Mr. Makara said. "He is not much hurt."

"Now you must heal," his wife said to him. "You must get off that leg, and rest, before the next hunting party comes."

We were so tired, Lanni and I, we could hardly talk. When we finished eating, Lanni politely put our bowls on the tray and wanted to take it out for Mrs. Makara, but she made a disapproving face. "You, too, must rest. I have called the helicar for you, for the morning. Now you wash and go to sleep. There is hot water for you."

I can't remember when I enjoyed soaking in a hot tub that much. It was a big metal basin, and true enough, a perfect blessing of hot water poured from the metal tap and rose around me. I wriggled and groaned with comfort, feeling much of the weariness wash away. On the other side of the tiled room, in her own basin, Lanni sank completely down, then rose up streaming, eyes squeezed shut, hair like seaweed over her face.

"Oh, this is living," Lanni said. "Maybe I ought to put in for duty up here."

"If only we could do that," I said. "But they've got their Councilmen, and if they need us they call, and we come. Or go. If you wanted to be a Preserve keeper, you'd have to be born into one of the families."

"I really wouldn't want so much isolation," Lanni admitted. "It was just momentary madness."

"Yarf," I barked, in understanding.

We were well rested by the time we caught the rocket flight that would connect with a bus to return us to the Academy. There was no question of sleeping on this trip. I had sort of changed my mind about going to a warm place on my leave, perhaps because Lanni talked with such enthusiasm of visiting her parents.

On the bus ride to the Academy we were still talking about our plans. "If my mother's home, I'll visit her," I said. "I'll go home anyway; I haven't played the cello in a long time and my fingers are stiff. A week of music would be wonderful."

"You're a funny combination," Lanni said. "All that muscle and action, and you play the cello."

"Don't forget the noseflute," I said dryly. Lanni had never said she was the brains of our team but she implied it sometimes, and I was a little tired of fielding these remarks.

"Oh, Roxy, I didn't mean that the way it sounded. But we did grow up very differently. I mean, my family was always old-fashioned. More like the frontier families now on the colony planets."

"Yes, I've heard they're very close-knit groups. I suppose they have to be, especially on Alpha, with the terrific temperature changes and huge deserts. They live isolated, like the Makaras, only more so, from what I've heard."

"It must be just as dangerous on Vogl, with all those bogs and volcanoes."

"Not to mention the creatures that weigh three tons and browse in the forests," I added. "Someday, I'm going there and see for myself."

Lanni sighed. At heart, she was a devoted Earth person. "It's only too likely. And with all their complaints and hostility toward us, there'll be real battles on both planets any day now. And right here, too. There was that Vogl demonstration in Africa Dominion last year when they burned out a whole city before they were done. All because they want to come to our schools."

"Well, I think they're entitled to it," I said. "How'd you like to be stuck up there in that climate, in a bog or forest, with no chance of being anything but a farmer?"

"Come on, Roxy, they make twice the money we do, and they feed us all. Our lives on Earth just about depend on Vogl agriculture and Alpha mining. They know that."

"Maybe it isn't enough. I'd hate to have to be an orthopedic surgeon just because my mother is. I'm not suited to it. All that finicky detail while a live body lies on a table in front of me. I can't imagine being forced into a profession against my will."

We continued to argue about it, good-naturedly enough, until the bus let us off at the Academy grounds. There wasn't a person in sight. We were due at Colonel Wayers's office right away, so we had no time to contemplate the familiarity of our training place. If we made the grade, there would be no formal

39

ceremony because trainees came back from the final test at different times, depending on how long it took to complete.

As we went up the front steps, I did wish that I felt more experienced, or different, or more confident. All we'd done was pull a dog up out of a hole in the ground, and in retrospect, it didn't seem enough to qualify either of us for Planet Patrol.

The Colonel wasn't in at the moment, so we sat on a bench in the hall to wait. Neither of us said a word. It was depressing.

At last he came briskly along, said to us, "Aha, come in. Sorry to have kept you waiting."

We perked up immediately. His tone was much more friendly and encouraging than we remembered.

He sat at his desk, opened our dossiers, said "Hmmm" to himself several times, turned pages, and sighed as if with utter boredom. I couldn't make out if it was an act or if he did it all without thinking about it.

"Yes," he said, looking up. "You've both got a week's leave before your first jobs. Tell Sergeant Mother if you want us to make any travel arrangements for you. If not, you're welcome to stay here. The next group of trainees doesn't come in until Friday."

We itched to be gone, but had to wait until we were dismissed. The Colonel turned more pages, gave us a cheery smile, and surprised us by saying, "Thank you both. You're a credit to the Academy, and we'll be watching you with pride."

"Sir!" we cried joyfully, and with thanks.

"That's all. Go along, will you?" he said, as we still stuck to the chairs, not knowing what to do. "There's no more formality, Officers. You are needed out there. Your job assignments will be sent to you."

"Home," Lanni said when we left his office. "How nice. Maybe we'll meet somewhere on a job, do you think? I did enjoy working with you."

"Me, too, Lanni. We're both up for psych check at one of the centers in six months, perhaps we can arrange to go to the same one."

Lanni had her belongings under her arm and was out of the building before I'd even spoken to Sergeant Mother, to give her my mailing address in Savannah and to arrange transport.

"Good luck, Officer," she wished me on my way out. I thought how many, many times she must have said that, how I was just one of hundreds of trained people going out to work wherever I was called. It made me sad and glad at the same time—sad because I wasn't anybody special, but glad because I could feel special to myself.

When I got home, it was so neat and deserted I could tell that Mom was on a visit or tour. Right away, I put through a video call to her office. The face of her secretary, Maxine, looked out at me. She smiled and said, "Dr. Rimidon's gone to a convention in Honolulu, and then she has a lecture in Helsinki. How long will you be home?"

"Just the week. Thanks, Maxine."

"I guess I better call you 'Officer' now?"

"After all these years, I'd be offended if you didn't go on calling me Roxy."

Her round and pleasant face continued to shine brightly on the video. "Roxy," she said, whispering. "I'm not supposed to say anything, but your mother's been proposed as head of the Bone Bank."

"No wonder she's busy! If I don't see her before I go, you must tell her I hope she makes it."

"Of course I will. Good luck, Patty."

We signed off, and I sat for a while, thinking about almost nothing. Then I unpacked my little bundle of belongings, realizing it wasn't the first time I'd had news of Mom only through a secretary. I didn't really need to talk to her, but it would have been nice.

I tuned my cello and practiced for a long time. Then I had

41

lunch and took the cello down to the Monorail Station. It was as if I'd never been to the Academy, riding among the crowds on the Monorail with the cello propped against my thigh, my arm around its neck, close as a pair of lovers, and the roofs and hazy blue sky going by outside.

I took the walkway over to the Repertory Dome, which stood like an inverted half-melon at the center of the city park. Although travel and other expenses were credited to my Patrol card when I was on duty, nothing was free when I was on leave, so I paid my way into the Rep Dome, the standard fee for performer and spectator alike. The door swished shut behind me and I was in the lighted lobby. As this was my home district I didn't need to look at the directory but automatically turned down the left-hand corridor.

Spoken Arts was on the other side of the Dome. The walls of the music theater that faced the corridor were composed of Kerr cells; when a performance was in progress or by the time casting was complete, the cells opaqued and darkened. Into them was set a casting plaque, and the first one I passed was blinking on and off: SECOND VIOLIN (GRADY QUARTET IN G MAJOR). I passed more walls until I came to the next lighted one.

The plaque read (BRAHM'S DOUBLE CONCERTO). Coming toward me along the corridor was a fellow of about fifteen, carrying his cello. We pretended not to see each other, but there was no help for us, since we met at the theater door at the same moment.

"Oh, come on," he begged me. "I cut physics just to get here on time."

The door opened before I could answer, and the conductor looked out. It was Maria Guayez, who knew me. "Roxy!" she cried. "You're just in time." She smiled at the boy and told him, "Georgi, you are not to come during school hours. You know that."

He gave me a very bitter look, picked up his cello, and went away. "Come in, come in," Maria said, taking hold of the neck of my cello very tenderly. "I am so glad to see you again. But you have not played for weeks. What must we listen to?"

Several of the musicians were familiar to me, as we had played together under Maria Guayez before. At one time my brother had thought himself in love with her. He would sit in the front row here and never take his eyes off Maria. She got tired of the puppy and sent him away very soon.

Although I'd had no practice for a long time, I didn't do too badly. A couple of times I came in late, and once the first violinist stuck her tongue out at me when I lost my place in the second movement.

Afterwards, Maria invited me to have dinner with her. We talked about music, about some of her own compositions, and about the new block poetry that was becoming popular. She advised me to spend an evening in Spoken Arts and take in some of the group poetry readings. "What better way to spend your leave?" she asked.

She was almost right. I spent most of my leave in the park or at various theaters in the Rep Dome. I had one video call from Mom. We exchanged greetings, travel notes, and regrets that we couldn't meet in person. "But I promise to be home on your next leave," Mom said, quickly adding, "if possible."

I'd never known her to make a promise, or any kind of arrangement, without a loophole for her escape. It used to upset me awfully when I was younger. By now I'd pretty much accepted it as a basic characteristic of hers.

My orders came through. I took one look and gave a whoop of glee, for I was being sent to a warm place with blue skies and sparkling water. So much for Lanni's prediction that I'd find myself on the Arctic seacoast. Interdominion Games were being held in Acapulco, which meant all their Councilmen were on duty and a number of Planet Patrol officers would be sent in for extra assistance.

I packed up my few personal things, put on my new uniform, and flew down to a fine, hot seashore for my first job a day earlier than necessary. Thoughts of being on a beach had been with me ever since I'd been in Asia Dominion hiking through snow and ice.

The long, narrow land bridge of Interdominion South separated America Dominion from the islands and southern land mass of Cuba Dominion. Cities there contained recreational parks and beaches, theaters and music arenas, the fields and stadia for the Games, and one of the three Planet Patrol Headquarters where every six months each of us went for physical and psychological examinations before returning to duty. Outside the cities of Interdominion South lay towns and industries, a school for Councilmen, and an Interdominion House of Meeting in its own park.

As soon as I arrived, I checked in at Planet Patrol Headquarters for my assigned room and possible mail. There was a greeting from Merle Doucette wishing me luck. I sent a similar message back to her, then rushed down to the beach in a shift.

I dropped the shift on the sand and plunged into the water where I floated and drifted for a while. After that, I stretched out on the sand. In half an hour I could acquire just that gold color of skin that matched my hair. For the moment, I hadn't a care in the world.

"Tanning nicely," a voice said. I opened my eyes, but whoever it was had already gone by. All I could see were the long, sinewy legs, probably those of a runner, striding up the beach.

44

It was kind of fun to lie out here like a tourist; the beach was one of the few places I could be out of uniform and anonymous.

"Tanning very nicely," I said aloud to the sky as I turned once again, a forearm across my brow to keep the sun's brilliance from blinding me. It was just this way that my brother and I would lie down together and watch the clouds move like phantom ships through blue space.

I thought of him now, and remembered him at ten, or twelve, practicing balance on fence tops, rock peaks, town curbs. He had phenomenal balance and was one of the youngest Tumblers to compete in senior Games. They called him Gyro Rim.

Competition between the separate Dominions was often savage. Once the Torch was lighted, the Games got under way, and for ten days every year swarms of young men and women contended with each other. Year round they were in perpetual training. Competition was tough, sometimes bloody, occasionally fatal. We worked off our Dominion problems, our trade battles, our border squabbles, through the Games.

Next year, for the first time, the colony athletes from Vogl and Alpha would compete. The expense of bringing them to Earth was high, but the price of the colonists' increasing resentment at being left out might be higher. At the last Interdominion session, it had been decided they should be allowed to compete with the rest of us. Who knew what marvelous skill might be developed out there on Vogl, with its swamps and waterways hidden under a quilt of hot mist? Or on Alpha, the first planet to be colonized.

As I lay on the beach, turning myself honeygold, I thought of the old myth that the cosmos was created from the mystic letters of the alphabet. Man, speaking his word, was moving outward. We still hadn't given up the old dream of meeting others who would speak some other alphabet, though as yet there was no indication any such beings existed.

Toes touched me softly. I turned my head to look up and opened one eye, squinting. A little, delicate, dark-skinned girl stood there grinning down at me. "Are you Officer Rimidon?" she asked.

"Yes," I said. I sat up, brushing the sand from my skin.

"I couldn't tell . . . you aren't in uniform."

I rolled to my knees and pulled on the beach shift. "Then how did you guess?" I asked.

"I didn't. I just poked everybody all the way down the beach until I got to you."

I looked back up the curve of blazing white sand and saw a lot of curious people staring at us. "And who are you?" I asked, thinking she was a very nervy child.

"Captain Wananga's daughter. She would like to see you in her office. You're a nice color."

"Thank you," I said, getting to my feet. "So are you." After all, I thought, she'd done the most practical thing, since she'd been sent to find me. Hardly anyone on the beach wore clothing, let alone identifying insignia. I followed her back up the beach. She kept tilting her head to look up at me and our smiles got warmer as we went. I revised my opinion of her from brat to smart kid to delightful child.

"I want to go to a Patty Academy, too," she said, as we turned onto a beautiful mosaic path leading to a moving walkway. "I want to be good at everything. Mother says I have to have more discipline, though."

"Why, you're only a kid," I said cheerfully. "How old are you?"

"Nine," she said with a big sigh. "Look at all the years I have to wait." She took my hand and guided me onto the walkway which would take us toward Planet Patrol Headquarters.

"Don't you think I ought to change into uniform?" I asked.

"Mother said you aren't on duty, so it's all right."

46

Then what the hell does Wananga want to drag me off the beach for? I wondered.

If I'd been prepared for the child's mother to be small, too, I was wrong. Captain Wananga stood six feet tall. She had a long, narrow skull on which the black hair curled into a tight cap, an aquiline nose, and black eyes. In the light blue summer Patrol uniform, she was breathtaking.

"I see Neeba found you," she said in an easy voice.

"Yes, ma'am."

"Sit down, why don't you, Officer." She sat down behind her desk and I sat opposite her, the cool light from the opaqued window on my face. Her elegant head and shoulders showed in silhouette against the window. She said, "I wanted to meet you, and brief you a bit, before you go on duty. You don't mind, do you? It is your personal free time."

"No, ma'am," I said, swallowing my annoyance.

"Those of us who are assigned to Games are those who can be spared from other areas and who have a record for keeping cool heads. Although the Councilmen handle most of the Games situations as they arise, we're not very popular around here at this time. At any rate, there cannot be any partiality shown for Planet Patrol members."

"I realize that." I wondered what she was talking about. My brother, perhaps? "Is this about my brother?" I asked.

"Brother?" she echoed. "I don't understand."

"Gyro Rim. He's competing here."

She curled her fingers up into her palms and I noticed that her left wrist was a little crooked. Planet Patrol must be very busy to call her back on active duty. And she didn't look more than thirty, though she had a child of nine. I was awfully curious. Thirty was the age at which most of us just begin to think of marriage and a family.

"Are you very attached to your brother?" she asked.

47

"I'm proud of him and I like to see him win, but he can't win all the time. He's only seventeen."

"Only! How old are you?"

"Eighteen."

She was thoughtfully silent for a moment. "Well, you see, they've dragged me out of my hidey-hole for this duty, in spite of the fact that I have an artificial arm bone."

"Is it the new porous plastic?"

She held out her wrist. "You're familiar with it? Unfortunately, mine was one of the very early jobs, as you can see."

"My mother's an orthopedic surgeon. She put in a new spine for my Uncle Wrexel last year. It's the first porous plastic spine ever done. He grows foodgreens in Interdominion North, in a glasshouse." I tried to restrain my smile, feeling she wouldn't appreciate a family joke, but since I'd already smiled I felt I'd better explain it. "It creaks in the cold climate. My uncle's plastic spine, I mean."

"And that's funny?" she demanded.

"Uncle Wrexel makes jokes about it. They tried to retire him, but he refused. So he gets around all right, and they have a special chair for him at work. He only creaks outdoors." I checked my giggle as well as I could. "He's busy hybridizing vegetables."

"Raul must know him," she said. "My husband's spent months revising the Standard Encyclopedia of Foodgreens. We carry pounds of reference film with us wherever we go. When I was called to duty here we came down together, and he disappeared into C for Cabbage. He did say he'd meet me for dinner, though." She rubbed her wrist and looked at it. "Creaks!" she snorted.

Then she changed and became brisk. "Officer, there have been rumors that some young people from Vogl may try to make trouble, though it is only rumor so far. Of course there are Vogl Council families here, but there's a group that has

48

threatened to come in and make trouble because they feel they should be competing this year. You must have heard some of this?"

"I've heard there's a group called Vogl Independents who want to establish their own Dominion and free themselves from Earth. There's plenty of the same talk from Alpha, too."

"There's an extreme Vogl group called Insurrectionists who create most of the trouble. There's quite enough tension and hair-trigger temper at the Games, between Dominion members, without dumping an outside group into our laps. We're supposed to keep an extra-sharp check on things. Patrol the Games at ease but keep a watchful eye on the practice pits and walkways. Needless to say, if there's trouble, and no Councilman is handy, you should take care of it. Have you seen your brother since you came down?"

"No ma'am. I thought it would be a good idea to stop off at the Tumblers' pit tomorrow and say hello. That way, he'll know I'm on duty, and we can stay out of each other's hair. I mean, I'd be sorry to have to mix it up with my own brother if he got into any trouble."

"Very sensible," nodded Captain Wananga. She thumbed a button on her desk. The door opened and Neeba came in and stood at attention, all three and a half feet of her, in front of her mother's desk.

Her mother said, "Time for you to go back to our quarters, and please remind your father he's to meet me for dinner." As Neeba was going out, Captain Wananga called, "And don't you dare stay up late again tonight!"

"No, ma'am," said Neeba, disappearing with a fiery grin.

"Oh, I like her," I said.

"She's a nice child, but wild. She wants to do everything right the first time and has no patience for learning or hard work."

"Does anyone, at nine?"

"I did," she snapped, looking me hard in the eyes.

I had no reply. The Captain packed up some microfiles that lay on her desk; she put them into a locker and turned the disc that secured it. "Well, you're not on duty," she said in a much softer voice. "Thank you for coming in. I'll see you, I'm sure, tomorrow, at Games."

"Yes, ma'am," I said, then added, "My Uncle Wrexel's just developed a yellow cucumber."

The Captain gave me such a droll look that I laughed. "Well, I thought your husband might like to know about it."

"But what good is a yellow cucumber?" she asked, amazed.

"It's got carotene, ma'am. Vitamin A."

"Oh, I see. Yes, Raul will be enchanted." Her lips twitched as if she wanted to laugh at all of us. "Thank you, Officer."

This time I was definitely dismissed. I still had time for another swim, a few more minutes on the beach in hot sunlight, and a walk to a cafeteria for some supper.

◆

PLONK! went the timer. I opened my eyes to morning light, feeling fine. I put on my open-collared summer Patrol shirt, gauze-weight pantaloons, socks, and boots, with the pantaloons tucked into the tops. Then I brushed my hair, gulped a hormone tab, and slapped my cap on. I should have had a haircut before coming down; the waves were growing long down the back of my neck. When I made Captain, I would damn well grow it down to my waist, as it had been before I went to the Academy. Then I could roll it up under the cap or let it down for off-duty, just as I pleased.

The low buildings were all polarized glass set into white or pastel walls. There was a good breeze coming in off the Pacific, the sun was bright, the walkways filling up. I got a quick breakfast and took the speedway through the city toward the

Games field and practice pits. I could have taken a heli but I wanted to see, smell, and feel as much as I could. The blue Patrol uniforms were scarce, though the beige shirts and shorts of Councilmen were everywhere.

A group of Hurdlers from Asia Dominion turned onto the speedway ahead of me. I could recognize them by that extra clump of muscle at the top of the thigh, which comes from pushing off from the ground for a high-speed jump. A little farther on, they were joined by a Hammer Relay team in the white and silver of Scandia Dominion. There's nothing more beautiful than people who feel healthy and walk happy. They made me enjoy the feel of myself—in top physical condition, hard-muscled, fast, ready for action. This morning I could easily jump over the moon.

I stopped off at the Sprinters' pit for a while, to watch them warm up. The walkways that ran above the pits were motionless, so that one could stand and look down. A ramp led down to each pit and there was a constant coming and going.

One of the Sprinters looked up, and I heard a hostile whisper: "Patrol! Patrol!" There were uneasy glances, as if I'd brought trouble in my pocket. I turned and went on.

In the middle distance of the field stood the pair of thirty-foot towers where the Tumbler judges would sit. Between them was strung the cable on which the round cage would rise with a Tumbler inside, the man or woman who was part dancer, part gymnast, and all nerve and coordination. Maybe I'd get a chance to watch Gyro up there. It would give me the same ache it always had, a combination of fear, admiration, and love.

I heard it again as I walked toward the Tumblers' pit: "Patrol!" It came from the lips of a young man standing with his Alpha family and watching the Tumblers. His father wore the white headscarf adapted from desert regions on Earth, and his mother wore a Kile fur belt. The young man had taken his identifying headscarf off and had tucked in into his belt. It looked as though he'd discarded more than a regional tradition. As I approached, he stared at me.

"Hi, Patty," he said. "You'll see me up in the cage next year."

His father touched him on the arm to quiet him, but he went right on. "I've been in training four years. Bet you I'm first, best, and winner next year."

He looked in good enough shape to give the other Tumblers real competition, even this year. I sort of saluted him, then turned away to look down into the Tumblers' pit. Four people were there, two of them in the blue stars of America Dominion.

A practice pole had been raised six feet above the ground, and a girl in the blue stars was whirling with one knee hooked around the pole. Her back was arched and both arms outflung; her speed increased until she was a whirling blur. In a few hours, she would do that in a cage which was slowly tumbling in any one of six directions, thirty feet above the ground. It moved in an established pattern which the Tumblers had to memorize. If a Tumbler forgot it, or lost balance, nearly always she could grab a bar of the cage and save herself. She was given one chance to return to the center pole and continue. Now and then a Tumbler missed, and fell through the cage.

I started down the steep ramp to the pit. "Patrol!" The Tumblers all turned to look at me as I stepped onto the sand. I found myself face to face with the nearest Tumbler. His nostrils flared with surprise. He had automatically gone into a semi-crouch and I, too, had the same reflex.

His reaction time had always been better than mine. While I stopped to think—I can let him put me down because I'm his sister . . . but I can't let him put me down because I'm Planet Patrol—Gyro reached out and snatched the cap from my head. He gave a whoop and hurled it past me to a friend. A series of gleeful exclamations came as they passed the cap between them. If I hadn't represented order and control it would have been just a silly kids' game. But I lost my head. With a yell of outrage, I reached out and pulled Gyro's hair, just as if we were still schoolkids at home.

He let out an answering yell and grabbed mine, drawing my head over to his shoulder. His friends had turned suddenly silent. Gyro was two inches taller than I. We both had the same coloring, the broad cheekbones, the wide lower lip inherited from our father. Father's temper bloomed in us, too.

"You . . . little . . . Patty," my brother growled. He gave my hair such a hauling I could have screamed. And then faster than I could think, he flipped me over and I came down with a thump on my back and he was sitting on my stomach with both hands raised in a gesture of gleeful triumph.

I rolled my eyes around at the faces which looked stern, and a little scared. The girl had come down off the pole and was standing behind my brother. She said, "Gyro, that's *Patrol*."

I did what I could. I said, "Ow!"

Somebody snickered. It flared into giggles which ran through the nervous group.

I said, "Ow, ow, that hurt!" and put my hands on my brother's shoulders. He leaned down and kissed me, then got up and helped me to my feet. The stares of the others became less strained.

"Rimidon!" came a voice of tremendous authority from the walkway above our heads. I looked up. There stood Captain Wananga.

"Good morning, ma'am," I said brightly. Someone put the cap into my hand, I slapped it against my hip to dust it off, and put it back on my head. I took my brother's arm and pulled him forward to my side. "I'm pleased to introduce my brother, Gyro Rim."

A long breath went around the circle. Someone laughed. Captain Wananga came down the ramp at a deliberately stately pace. The sun flashed from her boots and from her insignia.

"I'm delighted to meet you," she said to Gyro in a dry voice.

53

"I'd appreciate it if you'd treat our Officer a little less brotherly when she's in uniform. Rimidon, I'll see you in my office before dinner."

"Yes, ma'am," I said.

She departed with the same slow, stately gait.

"Roxy, I'm really sorry," Gyro said. "You know, in that first flash all I saw was the blue uniform, and then when I realized it was you, I couldn't resist it. I'm touchy anyhow. We've lost two Tumblers with strained muscles or tendons. There's just me and Debra to uphold the honor of America Dominion."

The other Tumblers had gone back to practice. We walked a little way away from them. "It's all right," I said. "It was my own fault. I stopped to think about you being my brother, or you'd never have put me down."

He said, "Oh, no? You're in fair shape, aren't you?"

"I'm fine. Have you been home lately? Mom may be named head of the Bone Bank."

"Yes, I heard. I was home last month. We've done all right, the three of us, haven't we? If you'll forgive the vulgar display of family pride."

We had been very close, especially the year Dad was killed. I could remember calling out the timing for Gyro as he worked out on the pole at the local arena. He had balance and courage very young; his incredible, continual flow from one figure into the next came with maturity.

"Will you do me a favor?" he asked as he gave the hair on the back of my neck an affectionate tug. "Stay out of my way here. I get along fine with everyone. You're not all that welcome in the pits, you Pattys. Wherever you are there's trouble, you know."

"The trouble is usually there first," I said bitterly. "But I know. I came down to see you, so you'd know I was around. Now we can keep away from each other, though I'll watch you in the cage, if I can."

"Good! I'm going to win," he said. Then he walked back to the pit. I went up the ramp and looked down. He was on the pole, hanging at arms' length: *one* two three, shift hands and reverse; *two* two three, shift hands and reverse; *three* two three, up into the air, a double somersault, and down to the pole, horizontal for an instant like a bird taking an air current, then whirling around with no grip, belly to the pole, speed and centrifugal force keeping him in place. The ache of admiration and love started again. I turned onto the walkway without looking back.

Farther along, I glanced down at the Swordsmen. There'd been a slight accident; blood showed on one man's arm. They wore face guards, padded vests, and shorts; they all had scarred arms. During Games they lost more blood than anyone, which was one reason they were so popular. Along with the Tumblers and Hammer Relay, Swordsmen drew the biggest and loudest crowds.

The sun was getting high and the stadium seats were filling up. From the pits rose the tension of waiting, the twanged nerves, the tight voices. There would be some down there who had already resigned themselves to failure. Now and then one of these would disappear before Games began, preferring social suicide to public shame, as if there was really any difference.

I was looking down into the pit where the Marathon Runners warmed up when several adults and a girl of about fifteen stopped near me to watch. I recognized their Vogl dress, the pants cut tight to fold in just below the knee. Wetboots were always worn outdoors on their planet; no one wanted sloshy pants, or the trouble of continually tucking the pants into boots and shaking them out again. Vogl people wore their tight pants wherever they went. After all, they were conquering a steaming, wet world and were justly proud of it.

When the family started on its way again the girl turned back toward me. She had light blue eyes which looked like ice. "Someday I'll go to your Academy," she said. Her hate was visible, like frost.

Her father gave a shocked exclamation and tried to pull her along with them, but even as she was being pulled backwards she went on at me: "I'm just as good as you are." By this time she was yelling and everyone on the walkway stopped to listen. "In five years the Academies will be full of us. Next year we'll eat up your little Games and then we'll fill up your Academies and then we'll have our own Patrol. Who needs all you Pattys from Earth?"

I kept right on walking at the same pace, following her. "When you come back, look me up when I'm off duty, and I'll show you around," I said.

Her mother, in an agony of embarrassment, said, "Please excuse her, Officer. The kids can't understand that travel is prohibitively expensive. They haven't got the patience to wait for the new space drive."

"It won't take long," I said. "You'll have your own Academies and your own Patrol."

"Stinking Patty!" the girl screamed at me, the frost forming tears in her eyes. They dragged her away, hushing her, and I was left feeling tired and sad. I knew what I was doing was right, and I hated to be hated for it.

The people of Alpha and Vogl were half a step outward from our solar system; not much of a distance, but a start on the way to the exploration of the universe. It gave them a prestige they never asked for, and the necessity for living up to a reputation as pioneers, another status step they never requested. Not too long from now they'd be in our position—holders of the jumping-off place for another stride outward.

◆

There was a deep sound, like the ocean pouring into a valley. It was the voice of the crowd as the Torch was lit. Games began. I could see men grouping for the Broad Jump, and I shaded my eyes against the brilliant light to watch the first of them take off with a huge surge of muscle, feet reaching out to land as far forward as possible.

Back behind me, from one of the pits I'd passed, came a scream. I whirled around. Athletes from several pits ran up onto the walkway. No Councilmen were in sight. I ran back, my boots thumping as hard as my heart. The scream had been horrible, and I could hear a following uproar. As I got closer to the Tumblers' pit I choked on my own heart.

Pushing down the ramp, I yelled, "Clear it! Clear it!" to get through the crowd.

The practice pole had snapped in two, hurling the girl, Debra like a pebble from a slingshot, to crash into the broad support of the walkway. Half her face was broken, and she was so covered with blood I couldn't determine the rest of the damage. Someone had already punched the emergency signal and an ambulance heli was coming down. Gyro sat on the ground with the girl in his arms. I felt for her pulse. It wasn't strong, but it was there.

"That leaves just me," Gyro said. His eyes were narrowed with shock. "Just me for all of America Dominion. And she was good . . . she was as good as I am. Now that leaves just me."

"Okay," I said. "Okay, it isn't the first time there's been only one competitor from a Dominion." I pulled Gyro up as the heli men put Debra on a stretcher. "Gyro, maybe there's a chance to find someone else."

"Not a chance, Roxy. There's not a chance. She was good, you know."

"Okay, stop it," I said roughly. The Tumblers' competition began in the afternoon, but I already knew one Tumbler who was in training. I took my brother by the arm. He was so dazed

57

he didn't resist. His white shirt with the blue stars was smeared with Debra's blood and he kept trying to brush it off, only spreading it more.

One of the pit officials came rushing down and I told him, "Get another practice pole up and this time see that it's a good one! There's going to be hell to pay for this!" Councilmen were all around by now, holding back the curious and the morbid.

Gyro followed me up the walkway. When we got away from the crowd I stopped him. I made some notes on my Patrol card, forced it into his hand, and gave him directions for following the correct speedway. "Go to Patrol Headquarters, to Captain Wananga's office, and wait for me there. Promise?"

He looked less shocked, and less brotherly. "What are you up to?" he asked.

"Just give me a chance. I don't know if it'll work. Go on! Get to her office and tell her what happened. I'll be there as soon as I can."

I got him started off, then broke into a jog-trot, hoping I could catch up to my group before they went into the stadium where it would take me all day to locate them. As the Tumblers weren't going up until afternoon, there might be a chance.

Quite a few Vogl and Alpha families were around because an Interdominion Meeting was scheduled to begin right after Games.

I caught up with one Alpha family but it was the wrong one, and I passed them at a lope. Several Councilmen called out offers of aid, or questions, when I passed them but I shook my head and ran on. The family I wanted was just entering the east gate of the stadium. I called out, afraid they'd go in and be lost to me.

"Tumbler! Hey, Alpha Tumbler!" I called, not knowing any other way to get his attention. He heard me all right, turning fast, shocked at being called that.

As I came up, his father swung around in front of him

protectively and faced me, his expression cold. I said, "I'd like to borrow your son for a little while, sir."

"Certainly not."

"Please. I want to take him to the Patrol office. I promise he'll not only be safe, but probably very welcome."

The young man stepped to his father's side. "What is it?" he asked. "What could you possibly want with me in a Patrol office?"

"I'd rather you heard it yourself from Gyro Rim," I said.

"Him! He's down in his practice pit."

"Please," I said, "we don't have much time." The man turned to his son and asked him, "Do you want to go and see what this is about?"

"I'll go," the son said.

He came along with me, hurrying as I was. "You really are a Tumbler, I hope," I said. "You weren't just making a big Alpha noise."

"What kind of fool do you take me for? Of course I'm a Tumbler."

"Got records of training and everything," I said, shoving him onto the walkway that moved toward the helis. I flagged a flyer and he opened the door of his heli for us. "Patrol Headquarters," I directed.

The flyer eyed the young Tumbler with his Alpha headscarf tucked into his belt but made no comment.

Neeba was standing outside the office door. "Officer, you certainly have stirred up something in there," she said. She opened the door and gestured us in grandly. Any other time I would have been amused by her manner.

Gyro was sitting in the corner when we came in. His nylon shirt had been rinsed out and was still damp, though drying on his body. Captain Wananga, standing before the window, snapped, "Siddown!" We did. A splendid showman, she marched up and down the office, giving off sparks of hellfire.

59

She moved with her chin jutted forward from her long neck, and each time she passed me she whipped her head around to give me a glare, then continued her forward march, about turn, forward march.

"I see you have a young man from Alpha," she said at last.

"Yes, ma'am. He's trained as a Tumbler. His records are available—"

"—within three hours, of course," she said, marching.

"No, of course not. But I thought if he were willing to compete for America Dominion—"

The young man bolted out of his chair. "Are you crazy?" he shouted. "What do you mean, America Dominion? You think I'm going to put on your big blue stars when I can come back next year for Alpha and mop you up?"

Gyro had been watching this whole circus with a sly, sharp expression.

"It's out of the question" Captain Wananga said. "You can't put an unregistered athlete into competition."

"Why not? Gyro asked. "It can't take your computer very long to file records on him. We have two Tumblers registered for Games, and one's in the hospital. Why not?

The Captain turned on me. "Damn it, Rimidon, what are you trying to do, futz my relays? We can't set a precedent like this. He's got to wait until next year and come in all nice and legal, and you know it!"

The Alpha youngster was looking at Gyro, his head cocked to one side. "You really want me in?" he asked Gyro.

"Well, first I want to see you in the practice pit, to see how good you are, and how fast you can memorize the tumble pattern. And if you're good, I want you in. If you can put aside the ghastly shame of wearing colors other than those of Alpha." My brother looked slyly at the headscarf in the other's belt.

"I'd give anything to get up in that cage," he said. "Anything.

60

I don't care if I'm wearing a helmet and Vogl bogshoes. Just to get up there and show you what I can do."

Captain Wananga asked him, "What's your name, Tumbler?"She sounded subterranean, like a volcano beginning to seethe.

"Tray Thomas."

"Well. Well, well." She sat at her desk and slammed the communicator with the heel of her hand. After a moment, she said into it, "General? We have a little problem in my office. Could you spare us ten minutes?" A pause, and in a softer voice she said, "Five minutes, then? Or shall we all pour down to your office?

"He'll be over," she said to us, and sat. I'd never seen anything so dangerous-looking as her stillness.

Tray Thomas sat beside my brother and asked, "How old are you?"

"Seventeen. And you?"

"Sixteen."

"Start us young, don't they?" Gyro remarked, and winked. But Tray sat with his fists on his knees, tense and absorbed in himself.

I was beginning to sweat at my own folly. If much more time passed, we couldn't get Tray registered for Games before the cage went up for the first time, not to mention giving him the practice essential to memorize the tumble pattern. And the General would have a fit at the whole idea. And the Alpha families would find it intolerable—one of their kids in an Earth Dominion competition.

In his own good time, the General did arrive. We all stood up but he waved us down. It took Captain Wananga only a few moments to fiill him in. As she spoke his face slowly darkened.

"Outrageous," the General said, turning around to look at me. "Don't you think we're having enough trouble with colony

61

malcontents?" He fingered the breast pocket of his Patrol shirt with his stubby fingers, and in a peculiar gesture drummed them on his chest.

"Yes, sir, but one of their quarrels is they haven't been allowed to compete."

He turned around several times, giving out warning flashes like a beacon, then stopped in front of Tray Thomas. "And you'll go along with this? Alpha-born, you'll compete for America Dominion?"

"Sure I will. I figure it's an extra practice session for me. Next year I'll be back again and I bet you I win for Alpha."

"Oh, indeed!" the General snorted. Athletes, like Planet Patrol members, are never noted for their modesty, but the General seemed to find Tray Thomas more immodest than customary.

He turned to the desk. "Wananga, can you get through to the computer people and get this mess in order, and recorded in time?"

"Yes, sir, I'm sure I can."

"Well, let's go," Gyro said, getting up quickly. "Come on, Tray, we've got plenty of work to do down in the pit."

Tray came over to me and said, "I'd appreciate it if you'd tell my family." He gave me their seat plate. "I ought to be competing for Alpha, so don't expect me to thank you, but I'm sure my mother will offer you her undying gratitude."

I wasn't at all sure of it. Very few mothers enjoy the spectacle of their sons tumbling in the cage for the first time. My own mother had seen Gyro only once, complimented him on his speed and grace, and never returned to watch him again.

That's the Patrol, the dirty jobs all the time. If I hurried to report to Tray's family I might even have time for lunch, then get back to a walkway near the cage towers and watch. I stood up.

"Siddown!" the General said. "I wouldn't like to think that

one of our Patrol members in any way sympathized with malcontents," he said.

I took a deep breath. "There's quite a difference between sympathy and action, sir."

"As you've so nicely shown us today," he retorted. "I suggest you be thoughtful, young woman." He bent a little at the waist to look down at me, quite serious and very sober-looking. "And I mean thoughtful, Officer. Be sure what your position is on every matter before you act." His heels squeaked on the polished floor as he turned and closed the door very softly behind him.

The silence grew long. When Captain Wananga was still, it was still as a rock, or a tower.

"Time's getting on," she said. "My cousin's in the Hammer Relay, so I'm going out to take a look. And Roxy, for God's sake don't tilt at any more windmills today, or tomorrow, or any of the ten days on duty. There's nothing wrong with your sympathies but you can't act so directly. You hear me? And I don't want to see you in this office again until the Games are over and you come here to say good-bye."

"Yes, ma'am," I said.

It was a very quick lunch. I had to cover half the stadium to find the Thomas family. They were incredulous. "You mean he's actually going up there?" Mr. Thomas asked.

"Oh, I can't watch," Mrs. Thomas said, riveting her eyes on the towers though the cage still rested on the ground with its gate open. I could see she wasn't going to take her eyes off the site until her son was safely down, winner or loser.

The Hammer Relay had just begun when I joined Captain Wananga on a walkway. The five men of the first team were strung out in a line about thirty meters apart across the big field. The first man took up the handle in his gloved hand; it

63

was attached to a short thong from which hung the round weight of the hammer ball. He took his stance, swung his shoulders and torso first right, then left, then turned in a full circle, gathering momentum. The hammer streaked from his hand toward the next man, also wearing padded gloves and armwraps, who had to catch it by the handle, then repeat the swing and throw the hammer to the next man in line. They were all tremendously agile and powerful. The team with the best time and no misses would be the winner.

You could hear the sound of the hammer, with its thong and handle streaming out like the tail of a comet behind it, and the *whuck* as it was checked in mid-air and snapped back. The fourth man missed. The groan of the crowd drowned out the sound of the hammer as it landed beyond him, sending up a shower of dirt and making a small crater where it hit.

The next team walked out, wearing the black zigzags of Africa Dominion. "My cousin's third from the front," Captain Wananga said.

"I suppose I won't get close enough to watch the Tumblers," I said.

"Here, stop grumbling." She reached into her belt pocket to take out a small black case, which she unfolded and extended.

"Sighters," I said happily.

"A present from Raul, my husband, though he uses them more than I do, for his field trips. Picks out all sorts of green eats at a distance instead of crawling around on his hands and knees after them."

She used the sighters to watch her cousin's team, which finished with good time. The third team, from Europa Dominion, came out.

The second man made a bad throw, the hammer streaked out low, hit the ground, rose into the air, and although the catcher had thrown himself on the ground he wasn't fast

64

man from Canada Dominion broke loose and jogged away, not even glancing back.

I still wanted to go down there but had no excuse to mix in; the Councilmen were holding onto elbows and wrists, shouting, or rather outshouting, the young men. Gyro was tossed out, landing on his knees and hands, then instantly springing to his feet. An angry circle surrounded Tray; they harangued him furiously. One of the Councilmen took Gyro's arm to steer him off the field, but my brother shook him away and plunged back through the circle to stand with Tray.

While the angry voices went on and on, the Councilmen stood alert. Even at the height of the fracas the circle with its central pair of Tumblers began to move off, for the officials were clearing the field and the women's High Jump was being prepared.

All at once, the whole young group turned and looked back toward the thirty-foot towers. I saw Tray salute the air where a little while before the cage had turned with him inside. Gyro, too, saluted that space, then the two Tumblers walked off the field together, the angry colony men slowly falling behind, gesticulating and still shouting, but now in argument with each other.

I put the folded sighters, which I'd been clutching in a damp hand, into my belt pocket and went back to duty on the walkways.

At the end of the day's Games, I went to the Captain's office and found Neeba. "Please give these to your mother," I said, handing over the sighters.

She asked, "Are you sad because your brother lost today?"

"No, love, not at all. He won last year, and there are two more days in the cage. And anyway, he'll have another try in six months."

I returned to my quarters and washed off the day's sweat

67

under hot water. I was sitting with the electric brush, working on my hair, when someone sounded the buzzer and I went to the door.

"Hi, sis," Gyro said. Tray stood just behind him. "How'd you like to go out with us?"

Tray was simply looking past me. He stood with his feet planted apart, thumbs hooked into his wide belt; a clean headscarf was settled on his brown hair. Both of them looked like swaggering, healthy fellows.

"Thanks, Gyro, but I've been on duty twelve hours and I need sleep."

"Okay. In case I don't see you for the rest of Games, Roxy, I'll say good-bye now. I'm going home for a week. Any messages?"

"Tell Mom I hope she makes head of the Bone Bank."

We hugged each other briefly, and Gyro backed off. Then he cocked his head at me and asked, "Do you know where your next assignment will be?"

"You know I can't talk about it. Hot, wet, steamy, and lots of fun. Okay?"

He grinned. "Okay. You can swim and fish in your leisure hours."

"Oh, sure," I said. "They mentioned that this morning, how I could fish and go swimming, and mingle with the tourists at the bar." After a pause, I said, "Good-bye, Tray. See you next year," and I held out my hand to him.

He lifted his chin. "Good-bye, Patty," he said, ignoring my hand. They both went off. I closed the door and went back to working on my hair, mostly for something to do. I'd have a light meal, and sleep early and long.

I was tucking my pantaloons into my boots when the buzzer went off again. Muttering at the interruption of my thoughts, which at that moment were about alphabets and cucumbers and how long my hair would grow in two months, I went and yanked the door open.

open. There were bird calls and a little breeze in the big banana leaves, but I never heard another sound until the foot came down on my throat. Not hard, just hard enough to pin me to the spot.

"Hallo," the person said.

I moved my eyes. He was tall, with a thin, black, bony face, and wore pale nylon pants and a sleeveless shirt. In one hand he held an island cutlass.

"Good morning," I croaked.

He gazed seriously down at me. The cutlass swung casually as his arm raised a little, then dropped back to his side.

"A nap?" he asked.

"Yes."

"Funny place for it. We have some nice hotels on the island. We don't often get tourists asleep in the middle of a plantation."

"You can see I'm not dressed as a tourist."

"Oh," he said, taking his foot from my throat. "We are used to seeing people in all kinds of costumes."

Yes, I thought, lying very still; some people have shown up in Planet Patrol uniforms, the best disguise if you want to move freely anywhere. It makes lots of trouble for everyone. I measured the distance from the ground to his cutlass hand, then let my muscles go lax. He had a good eye and could tell if I was lying here all hunched for a fight.

"You'd better come down to the house with me," he said.

"Whose house?"

"Mr. Marant's. You're lying under one of his banana trees."

The cutlass had come to full rest. I doubled up like a closing jackknife to get both hands on his cutlass wrist and kept going, head over heels, flinging him down behind me. I held on until his fingers released the hilt.

Holding the cutlass, I looked down at him. He lay so still I thought I'd damaged him. His eyes were closed. When he opened them I could see how angry he was. His eyes were sort

73

of maroon and his upper lip was pulled so tight it disappeared. "Damn neat," he said, but he didn't move.

"Please get up. We'll go down to Mr. Marant's as soon as the Sergeant arrives."

He got gingerly to his feet, rubbing his hip bone where he'd landed. "I think you're a real Patrol. I'm fifty-eight and no one has ever taken my cutlass from me."

One day I'd be fifty-eight and not so full of myself as I was now, so it seemed worth taking a chance. I turned the cutlass hilt first and offered it to him, saying, "I'm sorry, sir. But we're trained for just this kind of thing."

He looked down his nose at my offer. "No, Officer," he said. "You took it. You keep it until your Sergeant comes."

I sat down cross-legged with the cutlass on the ground in front of me, and after a moment, he sat down, too, opposite me. "You're a well-trained young woman," he said.

"Yes, sir. I have to be."

He looked up into the banana tree from which the bird had fled; he looked down at the soft ground where we sat. Sprout-lets from old banana roots were up at various levels around us. A hot, dappled sunlight made patterns on our heads and knees, and I felt its welcome warmth on my shoulders.

"The Sergeant you wait for is also a woman," he remarked.

The cutlass lay between us on the ground and I wondered if I should have made that noble gesture. "You have seen her," I said in the same offhand tone.

He looked into my eyes with such sharp perception I was sure no imposter could fool him. "At dawn I saw a woman in your blue uniform walk up into the mountain toward the Three Voices. That is some distance from here."

As far as I knew, Sergeant Krane and myself were the only legitimate Patrol members on the island at the time. Either the woman he'd seen was one of the counterfeits or my Sergeant was looking for me somewhere else.

"What are the Three Voices?" I asked.

"Where the waterfalls come down. Our power station is there."

Water power? I was baffled. "Can you direct me there?"

"No," he said. "But I could take you there."

In the ensuing silence I wondered if he wanted a bribe, or wanted to see my credentials, or if he were planning how to do away with me, or if he were merely as mystified as I.

"How many of the fake Patrol people have you seen?" I asked.

"I have not seen one. I have heard that two men and a woman came in a small boat from the Atlantic side claiming to be from our own Dominion. They disappeared into the interior." He jerked a thumb over his shoulder to the great mountains behind him where the clouds were gathering for the daily rain. Nearly three hundred inches per year drenched the mountain forests, although the coast had months of clear weather with only an afternoon shower now and then.

Leaving the cutlass on the ground, because I was unwilling to back out from my own foolhardiness, I stood up. "Will you take me to the Three Voices?"

Leaving the cutlass on the ground, with a glance of utter contempt that swept from its blade to my face, he also got to his feet. "If you wish," he said.

I followed him down the slope, past the trunks of the banana trees. New ones were rising from the old roots where last year's trees had been cut down after the crop was harvested. When we came to the road I saw a truck of a kind I didn't think still existed. It was powered by combustion—a monster mounted on huge tires. Most of the paint looked as if it had been blasted off. The body was made of bare, splintery boards. He got in behind the wheel and I ran around the truck and got in beside him.

"My name's Roxy Rimidon," I said.

75

"Yes, Officer," he answered, and put the truck noisily in gear. It must have had some kind of brakes, but we sailed down the curved road first on one slant and then on another, with a terrible combination of noise and stink. Now and then chunks of the old road broke off under the wheels and hit the underside of the cab with the sound of a gong. A couple of plantation autogyros flew over us during the ride. We passed through the center of a town, with its cocoa palms and flowering bromeliads in the central square. Pale pink and orange houses, with their cool slatted walls, made a geometric print on the hillsides in the bright air.

The road began to curve up again. We passed a similar vehicle on its way down, and both drivers honked a greeting. When we reached the top of the hill my driver reached under the dashboard and pulled out a speaker from a tangled nest of wires. I never saw anything so unkempt, but it worked.

He spoke a patois which I could not understand except for "Patrol," which stuck out like a shout several times. In a few minutes, a heli, with the blue insignia of Cuba Dominion, flew into sight above some flamboyant trees and went on ahead of us, flying very low. The combined sounds of truck and heli were deafening.

We went up one mountain, down the next, and into a grey mist. Rain-forest conditions appeared around us. There wasn't an inch of bare ground. One plant grew piggyback on another; the great limbs of old trees bristled with air plants. Everything dripped and steamed, and I could have sworn I felt mildew in my boots. They were constantly full of sweat.

The heli had come down and was standing in a small, lush valley just below the electric power station with its strange poles and wires and insulators. Two Councilmen in beige tropic shorts and shirts were waiting for us.

"Here she is," my driver said as I got out. "She wants to go up to the Three Voices. She is looking, perhaps, for another Patrol woman."

The two dark men were stiff-backed and polite, but nothing more. They turned and began to climb a steep trail and I followed, hearing the truck roar away behind us.

The trail was rough, jumbled with damp stones, slippery with mosses, and soon almost vertical. There was a dull thunder which increased as we climbed. I was getting that depressed and ominous feeling one gets from subsonics, or the approach of doom, and began to wonder if the thundering vibration accounted for all of it.

Sweat and mist poured down from my scalp and face. My uniform was drenched; my boots were scraped and stained with moss. The air was so moist it was like breathing through a sponge. The thunder grew louder, rumbling and roaring in my chest. The trail took a sharp turn between boulders, and we stood under tremendous cliffs.

I looked up hundreds of feet to where the water began its fall. It came down in three separate places to a foaming, boulder-filled pool below us. In the pool, belly up, floated a dead woman in a blue Patrol uniform.

My two companions simply stood looking at her. I went down carefully to the water, where I took off my boots and waded in. The great torrents roared down and a cool mist blew across my face. I caught the body by one leg and pulled it back toward the edge, got an arm under the hips, and lifted her out. She flopped wetly, one arm hanging into a crevice. Her cap was missing, but papers in her pocket were orders addressed to Sgt. Ann Krane. When I looked up, the Councilmen were watching me suspiciously.

"Ever see her before?" I asked.

"No," the young man said. "Never. Is she the real Planet Patrol?"

Of course, what he meant was: Are you real Planet Patrol?

"I'm not sure. Give me a moment more." I pulled her shirttails out and looked for the featherweight belt at her waist. Strapped to it was standard equipment, including the tiny watertight pouch which held a metal match. Hooked into the pocket of her jacket was a steel tube no bigger than the match. I'd never seen one before, and I took it out to examine it. Something appeared to be inside. I tried to get it apart but nothing budged. I put my thumb into a hairline crack, and for my trouble I got two blue sparks.

If it was a signaling device, which I thought it must be, I had just sent a message. Standing there I listened to the enormous thunder, saw those awesome tons of water pouring down the cliffs, and wondered who, or what, might appear in response.

If the corpse was not Sergeant Krane, then she was still around somewhere and I'd better find her. The Councilmen came down together, picked her up, and began to cart her off down the slippery trail. I hoped she was not my partner, for I didn't feel like going it alone, and felt even less like reporting the murder of a Planet Patrol Sergeant.

The Roseau Council had first called for Planet Patrol assistance when the counterfeit Patrol people had appeared, and then suspiciously vanished. At that same time, a shipment of young-growth banana roots, wrapped in island soil and packed in life-support crates for transport to Vogl, had been found hacked to pieces at the airport warehouse. The climate on some parts of Vogl, though wetter, was similar to that of the Cuba Dominion areas where bananas grew. Because Vogl was our great agricultural triumph, with fast-growing colonies on the waterways and in the wet forests, one shipment of new banana trees was to be exported to Vogl every three months for a year.

No one was sure yet how they would survive the trip, whether they would grow on such a planet, or even at what stage of growth it was best to ship them. Nevertheless hopes for success had been very high until the first shipment was totally destroyed before it even left the island.

◆

We were halfway down the trail, the two men with their dead, wet burden ahead of me, when I heard a heli coming across from the north of the island. I thought of the signal I must have sent and called out to them, "Let's get under cover."

We twisted off the path, stumbling among huge roots. My boots slipped in the juice of torn leaves. When I glanced back, before the growth could obscure my view, I saw that the men had dropped the body on the trail. Damn fools, to leave it out there in plain view. I kept bulling my way through vines, got cracked across the brow by a branch, and wondered if any poisonous snakes or insects were around. The heli came on over the tops of the trees. There was the sound of the triple vanes, the whine of a beam from a laser gun on high, and the backwash of scorching air from where it had hit.

When the sound of the heli grew faint, I began to crawl back toward the path. Where the body had lain there was a little pile of black ash, with a few wisps of smoke still rising sluggishly in the moist air.

What interested me was the view they may have had from the heli. Did they see only a Patrol uniform on a woman, or did they know who the woman was? If they held Sergeant Krane, and assumed they had just burned me, the best I could do was get out of uniform and blend into the background. Blending into the background would be a chore; big, blonde, and fair-skinned, I was one of three or four such women on the whole island.

The two Councilmen crawled out to join me. "My God," the young one said.

79

"A laser gun," the older one said. "They ought to be banned. Not even a Patrol should use them."

Except on special duty, no Patrol member carries a weapon. I looked sharply at the gas gun on his hip, the weapon Councilmen wear at all times, and he looked away from me quickly.

Walking onto the trail, I kicked and scattered the pile of ash until nothing could be seen but bootmarks. Taking the lead, I went down, slipping over wet rocks, with the two men behind me.

The Councilmen drove me to their office, where I should have been able to speak with the Council president, but he was off on his boat with some friends. I didn't feel like waiting hours for him to return, so I left and walked through the old part of town to the coast where my hotel was. It had been built recently and was very pleasant—a series of one-room units facing the hot, blue Caribbean. The ceilings were high and a band of slat ventilators ran around them where the walls joined. The slats on the sunny side automatically closed when the temperature rose while those on the shady side opened. Like most of the island buildings, the wall facing the sea was all slatted so that the room could be entirely opened on that side. During rains, and months of high humidity, an automatic switch locked the slats shut and turned on the cooling.

Although it was warm at noon, the humidity was low. I lay down for a comfortable nap, chuckled to sleep by some bird outside my room in a sweetsop tree. When I woke, it was mid-afternoon, and the clouds which always stretched like Mercator projections at the edge of the sea were beginning to mass in long horizontals. I had time for a swim. The lava sand, brilliant purple-black with grains of silica sparkling in it, was fiery hot. I sprinted across it and plunged into the water.

When I came out I saw a figure standing in the shade of a

80

cocoa palm. With my feet wet, the return trip over the blazing sand was not as bad. There stood my cutlass-carrying friend of the morning, in a white suit with a bright green scarf at his neck, looking cool in all senses of the word.

"Mr. Marant would like you to come to his house," he said.

"I must go to the Council office this afternoon."

"It is pleasant here on our island, isn't it?" he said, and gave a look at my dripping self, fresh from a swim like a tourist. I could understand that he thought I should be on the job rather than enjoying myself. He went on, "Mr. Marant has asked that you come to dinner."

Very good, I thought. It would give me a place to start. For all I knew, Marant was harboring Vogl malcontents, or bootlegging tobacco.

"I will call for you at eight," he said.

I thought of the new kyrene dress I'd brought down and asked in a scandalized voice, "In that truck?"

"No, Officer, in Mr. Marant's helicar."

"What's your name?" I asked.

"San' Clement," he said, and turned away, adding something in a patois, from which I heard the word "Officer" burst out, accompanied by a kind of laugh.

The Council president, Ian Toxetl, was in his office. He was a fat man with shrewd eyes and an agreeable smile.

"Naturally, we think it must be members of the Vogl Insurrectionists. Who else would do such a thing?" he asked. "The whole thing is stupid. If they want to be independent, and carry on free trade, which they must do for years to come, why wouldn't they welcome a new crop to grow? That is what puzzles us so much. And it's common knowledge that if the banana shipments are successful, we'll try cocoa, and perhaps guava too. There are so few native Vogl crops which are edible, they should welcome these shipments."

"If they're fanatics, and the Insurrectionists seem to be just that, there'd be no limit to what they would try. There's been so much loud talk about ship space used for food animals or agricultural equipment, and not enough space for people to travel—"

He interrupted me, saying mildly, "But Vogl is an agricultural planet. The first settlers understood that."

"Yes, sir, but there's a second generation and lots of Vogl families would like to send their children to our Universities. They resent the exclusion of their young people from our Planet Patrol Academies and the necessity for calling us from Earth to come troubleshooting for them, not to mention their exclusion from Games. Even though next year they'll be eligible, for the first time, for Games, the resentment will last years."

Mr. Toxetl picked up the carafe from his desk and poured a red drink into two glasses. Ice tinkled in the carafe, and the glasses frosted over. It looked delicious. I accepted my drink and sipped it. Sweet and tart, with a faint flavor of nutmeg. After the sip was swallowed, the small fire of a good rum began to burn.

"This is what you might call a small-town island," he said."We're happy here. We rarely need to call Patrol for anything. Most of us were delighted to help send our banana stock out for experimental growth on Vogl. It made us feel we had some part in human progress. You must be aware that the shipment was donated by various growers throughout the island."

"I know, and they must feel bitter about its destruction. At the moment, though, I'm most concerned with the dead woman, and with her identity. If she wasn't Sergeant Krane, I have to find out who she was, and where Krane is now."

"Do you want to call your headquarters? We have rather primitive equipment, just the undersea cable, but we can make contact for you."

"If you please. Then we can get on with the job you called us for."

He offered to refill my glass but I moved it away. "No, thanks, though it's very good."

"Ah, yes, you're from the north," he said whimsically. "I've been there several times. No one drinks in the office. Am I right?"

I couldn't help laughing. "Just about, sir. I guess it's only a matter of local custom."

"So it is," he agreed, and refilled his own glass. Then he turned to the switchboard and began putting through a call. It would take some time, with such equipment.

In half an hour, I'd made my report and received instructions to proceed on my own, which was just what I knew they'd tell me. They also gave me the information that two livestock freighters had been impounded at the Vogl spaceport and their crews held as "guests" while Vogl flight engineers and other specialists took over. It wasn't yet known whether this was the work of the rapidly growing Insurrectionist group or of one of the older dissident factions.

"The Three Voices," I said to Mr. Toxetl, "is a very impressive place."

"Perhaps now that you've seen it, you'll understand why we've resisted the nuclear stations for so long, in spite of being called backward."

"But the nuclear station needn't be put by the waterfalls, sir. It could be put on the coast, or almost anywhere else you please."

He spread his hands. In this century of total mobility, pride of place was a rare thing, but I thought the people of this island still felt it strongly. Mr. Toxetl said, "Yes, it is quaint of us, we are told. But some of us still believe the Three Voices are meant to supply us with all our power. It's sort of an arrangement between those whose forebears were born here and the spirit they believe inhabits the falls."

Perhaps it was quaint, but having been under the power of that spirit so recently I knew what he was talking about. The thundering downpour of the Three Voices didn't just generate electricity, it represented something more, something intangible. Once a nuclear station were established, and the power drawn from elsewhere, that part of the interior would be deserted. The spiritual strength would no longer be met, and matched, by man.

I went back to my hotel to get ready for dinner. The tiny patios in front of each unit were filling up with tourists sipping bright drinks or eating fruit served in long wooden scoops. One of the scoops had been put on my table and filled with limes, bananas, and a mango. A small, dark bird similar to the one I'd seen that morning was drilling a hole through the mango skin. I watched his performance. He had a fine meal and wobbled off after he'd stuffed himself. I cleaned out the well he'd drilled into the mango and ate the rest of the fruit before it could spoil.

After I put on the kyrene dress, which was a changeable red—running through dark orange to scarlet to shades of rose and lavender—I showed off my sophistication by putting in a ruby nose stud. It was uncomfortable, but everyone at home was wearing them. What bothered me most about it was that in artificial light I kept getting red gleams and flashes from the end of my own nose, and sometimes I found myself looking cross-eyed.

◆

San' Clement put the heli down on the hotel lawn at eight o'clock, when the sun was setting over the Caribbean in gorgeous splashes of color. The clouds had turned black and were piling up. We lifted up and flew along the coast as the light quickly faded.

San' Clement didn't seem hostile, but he was silent. During the ride I felt he had to struggle to keep quiet. This conflict he had with himself did nothing to make me feel more secure. He set the heli down on the slope in front of Marant's white-and-orange-slatted house, lamplight shining in stripes across the front of it. He left me at the front door, then vanished into the night.

The door was opened by Mr. Marant, a small man, who stood a few inches shorter than I. He had amber-colored skin and pure white hair, though he looked no older than thirty-five. "An Officer!" he said, laughing.

He held the door wide and beckoned me in. I followed him into a big front room which opened toward the sea. The sea was black by now, with only a few faint boat lights showing as if they were stars drifting loose in space. Two men and a woman, all casually dressed in light clothing, were sitting around with drinks. They went on chatting as we came in, though the woman looked up at me and made a quick assessment. The two men were pale and thin, with that soft, porous look produced by years in a steamy, hot climate.

On the coffee table lay the blue cap of a Planet Patrol sergeant. The three silver chevrons on the side of the cap shone in the lamplight. Wherever my Sergeant Krane was, she had lost her cap. So had the body in the pool. A moment of outrage and disgust made me speechless.

I picked up the cap and turned it in my hands.

Marant said, "One of my men found it this morning."

The woman put her drink down and sat back in her chair,

examining my face, or rather my nose stud, with considerable interest. She was about my own age and pretty, suntanned, and in good shape like an athlete.

Nothing was said, so I asked, "Who saw the woman in Patrol uniform go up toward the Three Voices?"

"I did," Marant answered. "San' Clement was driving me down from a neighbor near there, and we saw her. I knew Planet Patrol had been called in and was glad to see you were on the job. Provided she was not one of the people we suspect to be imposters. Isn't it a mystery?" He cocked his sharp white head to one side and looked expectantly at me.

I could feel eggshells crackling under my feet; it was no time to be clumsy. I sat down beside the other woman. Marant brought me a drink. It was the same red liquid Ian Toxetl had served me, but much stronger.

A flash of ruby from my nose made me turn my head slightly, allowing me another good look at the woman next to me. Something about the way she sat, the way her clothes fitted her, made me think of Games athletes, who were in perpetual training, spare and steely—and of the Vogl athletes who were already coming to Earth to train for the next Games.

"You're from Vogl," I said to her.

She picked up her drink and took a mouthful of it. "Yes. I'm a runner. I came here to train."

She could be telling the truth. There was hardly any land on Vogl which was not a bog, swamp, or wet forest; no good place for a distance runner to train. "Long distance?" I asked her.

"No, one hundred meters," she said. I thought she was lying, for she had the long, slim muscles of a dancer, not the sinewy ropes of a high-speed Sprinter.

"I'm Roxy Rimidon," I said, and extended my hand to her. She flinched from me, and to cover it she picked up her drink again and finished it off. Sergeant Krane's cap was on my knee.

I picked it up and folded it flat. "I'll return it to her family," I said. With a deep breath, I plunged in. "You don't by any chance have her ID? She wasn't wearing it."

It ran through my mind that last year's proposal to tattoo a Planet Patrol member's ID number on the inside of the thigh was a reasonable suggestion after all, though a total revolt of Patrol members had blown the idea to a powder.

After the shock of hesitation from all of them, except Marant who just gave a cold smile, one of the pale men reached into his pocket and brought out the disc with the brainprint code on it. He tossed it to me. I put it inside the folded cap, and continued to sit there and take little sips of my drink. There were sounds of activity from the kitchen so I supposed we were going to eat soon. Whether I'd be fed before slaughter was something I'd have to wait to find out.

There was no other way out than the door we'd come in by. The slats at the front of the house were sturdy, though I could probably go through them by getting a fast start and using all my weight. Of course, no one in the room was going to sit around while I made a hole in Marant's front wall and escaped.

Marant was sitting on a formidable lounge in the middle of the room. It was made of white zyron zigzagged all over with such brilliant turquoise that it was uncomfortable to look at. He sat like a doll, dead center in the lightning design, wearing the cold smile.

I asked him, "How did you get her up to the falls, when she was supposed to meet me miles away?"

"It wasn't hard. I pulled over to her on the road to my plantation and said I'd seen a Planet Patrol officer going up toward the falls. She took the bait like a shark."

I gritted my teeth. "Do you want to tell me what it's about, or shall I just guess?"

"We'd like your cooperation," Marant said. "I hope you won't be as stubborn as the Sergeant. Actually, she was the victim of an accident; we'd much prefer to have her alive and helpful. What kind of training do you women get, anyway?"

"Long, hard, tough training. Since we are only allowed to carry weapons on special duty, each individual must consider her whole self a form of weapon."

Marant said, "We found that out. I've one man with broken ribs and another opened up from shoulder to hip with his own knife. As I said, her death was an accident. She was simply uncontainable."

"It was wrong," the woman next to me suddenly said in a raging voice. "There was no use killing her, it was stupid."

"She was a good Patrolwoman," I said.

"And you?" the woman asked, leaning forward.

"Try me," I told her, and she was halfway out of her chair when Marant yelled, "Reba, sit down."

She did what he told her. I turned back to him and asked, "What do you get out of all this complicity?"

"Oh, I have some acreage on Vogl."

It made no sense to me, Vogl acreage being worth only what you could raise or grow on it, and here he owned a big plantation.

I tried questioning Reba again. "Are you really a runner?"

"No. I'm one of the Vogl Patrol. We're opening our own Academy. Why should we try to enter yours? We don't need Earth Patrol. Half of you fall into our bogs the first day out and have to be rescued. We'll have our own, and do a better job. But I don't believe in murder. Your Sergeant would still be alive if I'd been in charge."

She looked so murderous I wasn't sure I could believe that. Though I had no use for the methods used by these extremists, like many Earth people I did sympathize with the colonists who wanted their own Planet Patrol. There was no reason they shouldn't have it, and in fact, most of us knew it was planned for the future.

The Earth Planet Patrol Academies had been established for fifty years, and during that time the best methods of training had been worked out. Staff must have years of active duty behind them and the rule was a good one: Don't teach what you don't know or can't do.

The plan on Earth books called for Academy instructors to be sent to Vogl within the next five years, when it was expected the ships would have a new drive, making it faster and cheaper to send live cargo back and forth. The instructors would establish Academies in two Vogl cities and train qualified Vogl-born people to staff them.

"Well," I said impatiently. "And what has all this to do with bananas?"

Marant got up. He lifted a fruit scoop from a table; it held things that were large, egg-shaped, with a bluish rind. At one end, a few blue-green fibers sprouted. He brought the fruit across to me and began to peel off the rind with a small knife. The pulp was rosy-gold. It had a heady fragrance and my mouth watered. I took the fruit he offered and sat looking at it, remembering the Academy instructor who had said to me: "Your appetite will be the death of you one day." Today, perhaps?

Reba took the fruit from my hand and bit off a mouthful, chewed it slowly, and swallowed. Then she handed it back to me. "That's a reem, native to Vogl. It grows under the same conditions as bananas, pretty much, and we can't see any reason for growing bananas, which you have plenty of, when we can grow reems and export them to you for a lovely high price. Taste it. You'll see what I mean."

I took a bite. It was excellent, sweet as flute music, with the juice a cool cascade running into the corners of my mouth. I was very hungry, expecially since the smell of calolo soup had started to drift out from the kitchen. It took some self-control to put the rest of the uneaten fruit down.

"Do you mean to say you haven't discussed this openly with anyone?" I asked.

Marant replied, "Sure we have. First we, or I should say they—for I'm Earth-born no matter where my sympathies lie—were told that Earth would be delighted to make a fair trade. So many crates of bananas for so many crates of reems. Reems, by the way, do not flourish here. I've tried growing them on my plantation. Bananas, however, would grow very well on Vogl—so it was hardly a fair exchange Earth offered. Then someone got the brilliant idea of shipping out young banana stock so Vogl could grow bananas for themselves and for export to Earth. But we've already got lots of different people growing bananas here—the growers on Vogl would have to sell their banana crops for very low prices to compete with Earth's growers."

Reba added, "And bananas don't travel well. Not like reems. That rind protects them from bruises and extremes of hot and cold. Reems are cheaper to ship, easier to harvest, and what's more, we've got all of them and you don't have any! Earth just wants to keep reems off the market. They're against having any economic competition from a colony planet."

"It's a matter for the Trade Councils," I said. "Why impersonate Patrol members, commit murder, destroy a whole shipment of banana stock? You can't expect us to do business with you now."

One of the thin men said, "The reem crop is in the control of the Insurrectionists, and we'll use it as a political weapon. Those so-called Independents already tried talking fair, and nobody listened."

At that moment the door from the kitchen opened and a woman said, "Dinner."

Without a glance at me, everyone got up and moved to the table. Marant stood behind a chair and gestured me over. I went and was seated with them. Marant poured wine into our glasses, the calolo soup was served, and we began to eat. I felt I was sitting with a flock of the banana birds, the spoilers, a gulp here and a bite there, ruining a crop for everyone just to fill their own stomachs. Out of the whole group, only Reba seemed to have the genuine motive of wanting to help some of the other people on her home planet.

"If you'd only left Sergeant Krane alone," I said all of a sudden, surprising myself. "What do you expect from me now, after you've killed her?" I was so angry my stomach nearly rebelled at the food.

Reba said, "I had nothing to do with that. I would have stopped it. We did have plans for her. Now we'll use you instead. If you don't decide to help us, and I can see you won't, we'll cover your brain with one of our encephalotransfer units and find out what we need for our Patty training."

I was only a few months out of the Academy, and every element of my training was still fresh in my mind. If they had one of the encephalotransfer units, and I was sure they did, they could lift most of it from my head while I lay unprotesting. It would leave that part of my brain permanently blank, and since I would be too damaged for retraining, I'd have to find some easy and undemanding job when I wakened.

"We'd prefer you to teach us willingly," one of the men said. The two of them were like twins—thin, pale, with even, soft features. "You'd get the best accomodations, a high rank, and you'd be titular head of the first Vogl Patrol Academy. Not to mention"—he smiled and showed greenish teeth—"that many of our farmers would be glad to husband you. In real style."

"Thanks," I said. "If there's anything I like to choose for myself, it's a man." I finished the last spoonful of soup and added, "I suppose your graduates will be known as Vapors."

"They'll be Pattys, too," the man corrected me, with no show of temper.

"Can't you wait a few years for this to come about peacefully, with cooperation between both planets?"

Reba said, "Don't you think some of us are sick of being farmers? After all, farming's been forced on us for two generations. We've got lots of bright youngsters who want to be radio astronomers, or surgeons, and very few of them get the chance. Most of them are packed off to Aggie School and spend their lives tending hybrid goats or tanks of fish eggs. You say you want to choose a man for yourself. Didn't you choose your job, too?"

Yes, it was a valid argument. And no, they were doing it the worst way possible. It would bring disaster to Vogl.

I helped myself from the platter of fried iguana. Marant went around the table refilling our wineglasses. When he came to my side, he put his hand on my shoulder and said, "At least think it over. We can use you, and we can offer you a good deal in exchange. If you stay on Earth you'll never make a high rank before retiring. We can offer you a Captain's rank just to begin with. And don't worry, you can pick your own man, or a dozen of them. The Vogl boys are healthy and good-looking."

Pushing away my plate, I said, "Now you're offering me a stupid bribe. Two stupid bribes."

Reba threw her wine into my face and I kicked my chair backward as I got out of it, not without a regret for my kyrene dress.

She was as strong as I, in her wiry way, but I had ten pounds on her. She had long hair, while my blonde waves were cropped very short and didn't give her much to grab hold of. Her training was not as good as mine, but she made up for it with her speed. The skirt of my dress went first, got tangled around my ankles, and took me down. She jumped at me with both feet. I rolled out from under just in time. We grappled on the floor for a moment before separating and getting up again. I was satisfied to see I'd ruined her dress, too. The bodice hung in tatters around her waist. I bent and made a feint for her legs, coming up with my shoulder under her chin. I heard her teeth crack together.

Reba was wearing hard sandals and had a tremendous kick; twice she nearly got me in the face with one heel, but the second time I grabbed hold while her leg was in the air, and she went over backwards onto the white and turquoise lounge. I heard a crack as the arm of the lounge gave way, and another as I landed full force on her.

Someone with incredible strength pulled me back and held me, with a knife at my throat. The two pale men gripped Reba and held her in place. "Damn you," Marant said into my ear. "I had that lounge shipped from Scandia Dominion and you've ruined it."

My laugh was little more than a gurgle.

"You're so conceited," Reba said to him scornfully. "No wonder they found you easy."

"Shut up," one of the men said to her. "He's worked hard and we need him."

"Will you stop fighting?" Marant said to me.

"If she will."

He released me cautiously. The rags of our clothing lay on the floor and my ruby nose stud was gone, leaving the nostril sore. I looked again at those slats opening toward the sea. There hadn't been a sound from outside since I got out of the heli and it must still be parked there. It wasn't going to be much fun going headfirst through the wall of the house, if I could manage it at all. And then, if San' Clement was guarding the heli, where would I go?

I twisted away from Marant and began to stroll around the room, rubbing the spots on my arms and shoulders that hurt. I came to a stop where the slat frame did not cross, and where it

93

might be easier to break through the wall. I knew I had to try it.

"Here," one of the men said, and tossed his jacket to me. I let it fall on the floor.

"Thanks, but it's warm," I said.

Marant eyed me. "Officer," he said, "if they build them all like you at the Academies, Vogl will have to go some to match you."

I looked sideways at him, as though the compliment had pleased me, and shifted my weight as though to show myself off. Then I took off from a standing start, headfirst, with my shoulders hunched. At the last instant I turned my right shoulder to take the brunt of the slats. They gave with a shriek and splintering, and I was on my feet again and running down the grass toward the shadowy mass of the heli, praying that San' Clement had gone home.

There was the hiss of a gas gun, and the hard sound of some other hand weapon as I ran in front of the heli to get around to the driver's side. The door was open, and as I put my foot on the step, a thin, cold hand, black as the night, took my arm and pulled me up and inside.

I fell across San' Clement's knees as the engine protested, groaned, and was revved up without mercy. We went straight up, then he worked it into its high speed and we began moving down the coast toward Roseau.

I wriggled over to the other side of the seat. My shoulder hurt and was bloody. The night air blowing through the vents chilled my skin quickly. I looked over at San' Clement but he said not one word.

"Were you waiting for me?" I asked.

"They have another heli. With a laser gun," San' Clement said. "We have only a little start. Where shall I put you down?"

"Can you get me near the Council office?"

"I will try." He was quiet again, and then as the lights of Roseau showed in the distance on the coast he said, "I worked all my life for Marant. I'm his foreman."

94

"Now you're out of a job. What will you do?"

"I have a house, and a few cocoa trees. Four sons and four grandchildren. It is not so bad. If we get to Roseau."

The lights of the second heli were visible behind us. "Has it got more power than this one? And do you have a transmitter?"

"It's fixed to send and receive only on their wavelength."

"How far are we from Roseau?"

"Half a mile, maybe. Look down. You can see we're over cleared land."

"Then put us down. I'll run for it, and you get under cover. They'll follow me, not you."

"You cannot outrun them for half a mile, Officer."

"I can try."

I saw his teeth shine as he smiled. "Oh, that is good. From the only one who could take my cutlass from me. No one can outrun a laser gun."

"They can't afford to burn the town. Put us down, San' Clement, and you take cover. I'll make it somehow."

We started going down. On his side of the seat, San' Clement was going through some vigorous contortions, getting out of his white jacket, then out of the dark shirt he wore under it. He tossed me the shirt. "Wear it, you show up like a fish belly," he said.

He put the heli down near a group of large flat-topped trees. The other heli was already coming down after us. We tumbled out. I ran—not toward the trees, which they'd expect me to head for, but across open ground, guessing I wasn't yet in range of their gun. It was a close guess. As I turned into the first street the laser gun scorched the ground only a few feet behind me. At least San' Clement had a chance to get out of the way.

The first fence was low and gave me no trouble; then, as I cut along behind the houses, there was a series of them. Several of them were high fences with no foothold, which slowed me

95

down. I had tied the ends of San' Clement's shirt around my waist, and was unhappily aware of the white flash of my legs going over the tops of fences. The heli was cruising not far away, and they probably had a light which they could use to spot me, if they dared use it right over town.

They dared. They put the spot on, and it made a light like white noon over a fifteen-foot area. It began to swing slowly across the grounds in back of the houses, coming closer to where I was. I was at the rear door of a small home. Inside, there was music playing, and I heard people talking. As the light charged toward my heels I walked into their kitchen, and right through. The music went on though the voices stopped dead. I made it to the front door when someone came out of his shock and yelled, then threw a bottle after me. It grazed the back of my neck as I plunged out the front door into the street. I ran between two houses on the other side.

The swathe of light crossed the street just after me, and then swooped back and circled over the house I'd left. When I got into the next street, I looked back and saw the heli low over the roof, and someone climbing down the ladder that hung from it into the backyard.

I hit the center of town at a run. Startled groups of people dispersed as I came along, heading for the Council office. I hoped Ian Toxetl was in.

He was tilted back in his chair taking a snooze when I burst in. At first he had no idea who I was, and he looked bewildered. Then he said, "You're some sight. What has happened?"

"Get me that contact through to Headquarters and I'll tell you, or you can listen in," I said. "And I'd like one of those red drinks, please. I'm thirsty."

He gestured to the carafe on his desk and I helped myself. His two Councilmen ran into the office and skidded to a stop, one on each side of me. Toxetl made a motion which caused them to back off and stand guard on each side of the door.

"Just the two of you in Roseau?" I asked.

"We're enough," the younger man said.

When Toxetl sat back in his chair, waiting for the connection to go through, I gave him a tightly condensed version of the story. He sent the Councilmen out after the man who'd come down from the heli, and they ran out with their gas guns drawn, which was enough to alarm everyone in town.

"Well, you've had a day," Mr. Toxetl said comfortably. "Why don't you sit down?"

"Got the fidgets, sir. Let me make my report and get this finished. I can't stand to have those people loose. Though I'd put in a good word for the woman, Reba. She wasn't responsible for Sergeant Krane's death. And if they're going to have their own Academies, they'll need women like her. Marant's your concern, I guess."

He lowered his lids, dropped his plump chin on his chest, and spread out his hands. "Yes, Council will take care of him. They can't get far in such a small heli, only over to another island or so." He leisurely put through a radio call to the office on the Cuba Dominion mainland.

By the time my connection with Headquarters came through, the two Councilmen were back with one of the Vogl men held between them. His face was bruised and he was missing a front tooth.

I was in the middle of my report when a light started to flash on the board. Mr. Toxetl reached over my shoulder to remove one of the plugs, and when I swung around to get out of his way I also took out the plug in front of me. I'd never handled this kind of communication before, and from the look on his face I could see I'd done something wrong.

He took his call and replaced the plug in its socket. Then he

97

said, "The heli ran out of fuel just short of the next island. The occupants were picked up by a Council boat, alive and kicking quite a lot. Who were you talking to, Officer?"

"Colonel Cohen."

"Poor Colonel Cohen," Mr. Toxetl murmured. "I'm sure he never had an officer hang up on him before."

"Is that what I did?"

He smiled kindly. "Yes, you disconnected." A light was flashing rapidly on the board. Mr. Toxetl moved the plug and took the speaker from me. "Yes," he said into it. "Yes, we've had a lot of trouble on this line, Colonel. Officer Rimidon's already scolded me for it. Here she is," and he winked at me and returned the speaker so I could complete my report.

The younger Councilman gave me a ride to my hotel. I was glad to get into the quiet, breezy room and wash the blood from the cuts on my shoulder. It was bruised, turning black and yellow. I'd bled all over San' Clement's shirt, so I washed that out and hung it to dry. Then I turned in and fell asleep in the time it takes for two breaths.

In the morning, I ate breakfast on the patio. The little banana bird was there, perched on the back of a chair. I pushed my plate toward his edge of the table, with a slice of banana on it, and watched him hop over. Standing on the rim of the plate, he pecked rapidly at the fruit, now and then giving me a smart look from one eye or the other.

Dressed, with my kit packed, I stopped off at the Council office for San' Clement's address. The older of the Councilmen gave me a ride to the edge of town, where he dropped me off into the care of his cousin, who had a scooter car. The cousin gave me a long ride and passed me on to his brother-in-law, who had one of the old trucks. Little by little I went back into the interior—from the clear blue coast up through the hills of banana and cocoa plantations and into the misty mountains where the daily rain clouds were gathering.

San' Clement lived in a white and pale-blue house with a garden of orange and red blossoming bromeliads surrounding it. The air was full of wet mist, and in the near distance a thunderous roar sounded. I took his folded, clean shirt from my kit and carried it up to the door. San' Clement opened it.

"Good morning, sir," I said. "Thanks for the loan of your shirt."

His wife came out and looked at me, wide-eyed. "You are young," she said in amazement.

I looked over the roof of their house toward the towering mountain tops. The Three Voices were over there; San' Clement lived enclosed within the constant rumble and thunder.

He said, "Yes, the waters come down just over there in back of us. You're welcome for the shirt."

"I wanted to say good-bye, and thanks for your help."

He smiled slightly and turned his head a bit. I knew he was listening to the waterfalls. He didn't say anything else, so I went back to the truck and was relayed down to the coast, where in a few hours I'd get my flight out. Perhaps a few days off, if Colonel Cohen would allow it.

I had a word to say to him about Vogl, and a request to speak for Vogl at the next Interdominion Meeting, although that was more than two months off. It seemed to me it was about time to space-freight a few less goats and sacks of seed and a few more people—young ones, full of vigor and new ideas—going both ways, to Earth and Vogl. It was true I was a new Planet Patrol officer, and I was only nineteen, but everyone is allowed a voice at Interdominion Meetings, a chance to speak for or against any decision. I thought it was time some of us got up and spoke.

If you asked ten people to plan their ideal city, and combined the ten results into one, you'd have a city much like Grandview. The only thing the ten people seemed to have agreed on was a need for open spaces and parks; Grandview had many of these, green with lovely rich turf growing from the red clay soil. Some of the parks were domed, all-weather play places. The largest, known locally as Centerpiece, had a Monorail Station at its hub. To the east, where clean blocks of three-story buildings spread out, you would suspect you were near the sea only on hazy mornings although Grandview was just a few miles inland from the Atlantic coast, not far from Savannah.

I took the Monorail toward the Medical Complex on the north side of town. There were not many passengers and my view of the clean new city was unobstructed.

A directory was posted in front of the central building of the Complex, so it didn't take me long to locate my mother's new office in the Bone Bank. I took the walkway over to her building and went up to the top floor. She was lucky to be on that floor, for she would have a view of the whole area from her windows. She always liked to look away at distances. Perhaps it was because she'd lived so long on the coast and everyday she had looked out to sea to where my father was farming the waters of the continental shelf up until the day he had died.

She was bending over a holographic projection of a spinal fusion, clucking her tongue. I could swear she hadn't moved since I'd seen her in Savannah the year before, but of course she'd been busy as always.

She hadn't heard me open the door, so I paused to look at her: a woman as tall as me, light brown hair streaked with pure silver on both sides, the snub, sensuous face of a big cat. I just stood for a moment, admiring her.

"Mm?" she twisted around to look at me. "Roxy! My God, Roxy!" We ran at each other. I bumped her nose with my forehead as we swung each other around. "Oh, look at you," she said. "How long can you stay?"

"Only a few days. I don't have an assignment, I have something to do on my own. I want to talk to you about it, but first I want to take you to dinner. We'll have a bottle of wine and a good halibut steak."

"Halibut steak has gotten very expensive," my mother said, putting the holograph away. "You let me buy the dinner, and you can take care of the wine."

We stood there smiling foolishly, admiring each other. "You look wonderful," she said to me.

"So do you. Are you courting someone?"

"I'm too busy for that here at the Bone Bank."

"Oh, you're still using old bones."

She laughed and got her coat from the rack in the corner. "We still do, sometimes, for certain jobs, especially the temporary ones. Would you like to see the lab?"

"No," I said. "I'm not interested in the lab just now. I've only got a couple of days and I want to talk with you before I go to the Meeting at Interdominion North."

"Oh?" She looked curiously at me, and for the first time I got that cold gimlet look which she usually reserved for a bit of bone or chunk of porous synthetic. "Will you be stopping off to see Wrexel?"

"Part of the problem is I don't want to embarrass the family."

"Oh, you're not in trouble," she said in a voice of exasperation. "Really, Roxy, I hope you didn't come here expecting me to bail you out of some jam?"

"No, I didn't. I came because I need to talk with someone sensible, but I can shut up or go elsewhere."

"I'm the most sensible person you know," she said. "I'm sorry if I was short with you, but I've been desperately busy."

She was walking toward the door, buttoning her coat, when the door opened and a big man with white hair came in. He said her name, "Mahiri!" and kissed her on the cheek.

She said, "Take it easy, Jack."

Then he saw me, in my Planet Patrol uniform, and asked, "What's wrong?"

"Nothing," Mom said. "I'd like to present my daughter, Officer Roxy Rimidon. Jack Santiago."

"You scared me," he said with a big grin, coming over to shake my hand. He must have been about sixty, very handsome and full of life. I was glad to meet him, and I wished he would go away.

"Well, Mahiri," he said, "I rushed in to catch you before you went home."

"You just caught me. Roxy and I are going to dinner."

Oh, please don't ask him, I silently implored her, knowing my mother so well, but she said to him, "Would you like to come along?"

"I'd love to. I came in to ask you to have dinner."

Smiling with satisfaction, my mother tucked her hand into the crook of his arm and they went out together, not even looking to see if I were trailing them. I stumped along behind as mad as a ten-year-old, and ashamed of my feelings. Yes, indeed, I said to myself, it's about time some handsome, lively man just like this one married her. Then I'd always know where she was, and she'd always be there when I needed her. Infant Roxy Rimidon, howling for Mama, I jeered at myself. I hadn't needed her for ten years, and she knew it.

Jack Santiago took care of the whole dinner, including the wine. He was such a charming man it was easy to be pleasant, though I hardly got a word in edgewise before dessert.

Mom finally got around to me, and asked, "Have you ever seen Merle Doucette again?"

"Not since we left the Academy. But I had a note from her. She's already made corporal, and expects to go off to Vogl."

"I understand there's a lot of trouble with some Vogl groups," Jack said. "She'll have her hands full."

"Yes, I guess so," I said, thinking: Dear Jack, you are nice, but won't you go away now? He didn't, though. He kept us company right through the pot de crème au chocolat and little cups of hot Sangrada we finished with. Finally Mom said goodnight to him, and we went up to the Monorail.

"Don't you live near the Complex?" I asked her.

"One of the privileges of my new office is that I can live wherever I please," she said. "It's only a few minutes away, really, but it's right at the end of the line." We swooped and dipped along with a tremendous view of the dancing city lights through the windows.

As soon as we stepped out I could smell the sea, and standing there with my mother the shock of nostalgia almost undid me.

"Come on," she said, taking my hand. She had three lovely rooms on a bluff looking out over the water. And best of all there was a real sand-and-stone path from the walkway to her door. "I waited six months for this place to become vacant. I really hated living inland."

"I know," I said, more in sympathy than she realized. We kicked off shoes and boots and sat down in the living room. I had planned to sneak up gently on my subject, but having been bottled up all evening I just spilled it out in a hurry.

◆

"So you see, I don't want to embarrass the family," I finished up, "but I feel so strongly that we're wrong. I have to go to the Meeting and speak for Vogl. Any situation which drives people to such insane extremes is wrong and needs to be changed."

"In other words, you think it's more important to bring young colonists into our schools and training centers than to ship out agricultural equipment and ship back crops which support the colonists' economy. It's grand in theory, darling, but five or six years from now what will you say to the Vogl farmers whose crops have failed? What will you say to the hungry children?"

"I don't propose we stop sending seed crops and equipment, only that we balance the shipments. We're forcing the Vogl economy to grow and flourish because we get so much out of it—who are we fooling? It's as much if not more for Earth's benefit. And it isn't paying off. We've got more and more bitter and resentful people joining the Vogl Insurrectionists, and the resentment is spreading to Alpha, too."

She drew her feet up and settled more comfortably on the couch. "Look darling, you're only nineteen, but you are in the Planet Patrol. Sworn to keep the law and contain the mob and all that. And now you're going to an Interdominion Meeting to step out in front of all the Dominion presidents and tell them the law is wrong and the order can't be kept."

"Yes," I said. "That's what I'm going to do, because that's the way I feel."

She closed her eyes and rubbed the back of her neck with one hand. I said, "We were always liberal in our family and we always spoke up when we felt it was necessary."

I could see her swallow. I had dumped it all on her pretty fast. It was not that I was asking her permission—that would have been absurd for us both—only that I wanted her warned of what I was going to do, and hoped she would understand.

"Do you want to talk about your problems?" I offered.

"No, I do not," she snapped.

"I like Jack Santiago," I said.

Her eyes flashed with rage. "Don't you dare meddle in my private life," she said. "Jack's a sweet, lovely man, and the most awful bore I ever met."

She got up and asked, "Would you like a cup of tea before we go to sleep?" She turned on the video to catch the news, then went to the kitchen. I sat feeling tired and downcast, and looked at the face on the screen: General Bistrup—hard, powerful, vital, a man with the force of a tidal wave—was demanding, as usual, that the malcontents be dealt with severely, that the colony economy come first, before every-thing. As usual, in the same voice which had been coming over the video for more than a year, General Bistrup announced that young people could not think ahead, could not see far enough into the future to be allowed a voice in Dominion planning. You bloody old bore, I said to myself. Yet he was very persuasive.

Mom came in with two cups of purly tea, and we sat and sipped and listened to General Bistrup call for control, for logic, for sanity. "He's quite a man," Mom said.

Since I couldn't admire him that much, I kept quiet.

"He'll be at the Interdominion meeting," she said casually. "Will you address every word of your plea to him?" And she gave me a rather sly, sideways look, to see how I'd take that.

"I know what I'm up against. He has a golden tongue, though, hasn't he?"

"He's very intelligent. And he's deeply concerned with the future of all of us, Roxy. He is not selfish, or seeking power for himself."

Astonished, I asked, "Do you know him personally?"

"Yes, quite well. I put in his left kneecap."

I gave an uncontrollable whoop of laughter. From coast to coast there was hardly a patella or radius or spinal fusion my mother, Dr. Mahiri Rimidon, had not had a hand in. Or so it seemed to me at that moment.

"You'd better get some sleep, and I need mine," Mom said. "As far as your Uncle Wrexel goes, I think he'd be very hurt if you didn't stop off to see his glasshouses and have a chat with him. He was always fond of you and Gyro, and he won't be in the least embarrassed by anything you say. If I know him, he'll be delighted with your nerve."

We stood up, and Mom came over to me and took both my hands gently in hers. "Roxy, darling, they'll probably cut you to little bits, but I'll be thinking of you and mentally holding your hand, in spite of the fact that I disagree with you entirely." She smiled at me. "You're a scale off the old fish," she said, as she so often had in the past, when all in the world I wanted to do was go down to the shelf farm with my father.

We were settling down to sleep when I asked her, "Does Uncle Wrexel's spine still creak in the cold?"

"I'll thank you not to remind me of one of my bitterest failures. But he doesn't go out much, and they keep him nice and comfortable in his office."

"It wasn't a failure, Mom. It just had musical side effects."

"Oh, shut up," she said.

◆

I rehearsed my grand speeches as we headed northeast across the Atlantic toward the snow- and ice-covered land mass of Interdominion North. As we neared the port I felt frost entering me and knew it was a reaction to being so keyed up. I kept seeing in my mind's eye the face of Gen. Marion Bistrup, and I kept disciplining myself not to be upset by it.

We came down close enough to see the cream-colored domes of the towns, nicknamed Fomedoms, below us. The sea was silver, with long, moving rivers of light working across its surface toward the shore. It was very cold and beautiful, and not at all like the southern waters I'd grown up near. There were still parts of this planet I didn't know, although that didn't lessen my desire to get off this planet and see the rest of the known universe. Probably I'd get my wish, and wind up on a Vogl farm knee-deep in steamy kelp for the next ten years.

A bus with snow treads took us to the hotel. I would have to sign in before I could look up my Uncle Wrexel. I also wanted to register for the Meeting. Anyone could attend an Interdominion Meeting, but if you wanted to get up and speak, you had to sign your name in a register and sit in a special section which gave you access to the floor.

Off duty I didn't need to wear my uniform, but I had brought it. I couldn't decide whether I should wear it or not. I was afraid if I didn't wear it, I would be accused of trying to speak as a private citizen and a Patrol member is not a private citizen. That's understood even by small children. Patrol members belong to their planet and its people. Anyhow, I signed in as Officer Roxy Rimidon and saw it posted on the wall plate where guests were listed.

I got myself settled in my room, with my uniform hung neatly in the closet, and then went to inquire about the glasshouses. "Take a jitney," I was advised. "They run every twenty minutes."

The jitneys, small and as lightweight as toys, seated six people in addition to the driver. As we rode along we kept sinking, rising up over mounds, and sinking again. It was a strange feeling. The short day was coming to an end and all around the snow was streaked with blue ink where the shadows were visibly lengthening. The glass towers were awash with a tangerine fire, and nothing could be seen through its glow. I had to imagine the conveyor belts carrying the plants all the way up to the top, then down, then up, ceaselessly.

It was only a short walk from the jitney stop to the sealed door of the office building at the base of the glass tower, but it gave me an absolutely desolate feeling and I imagined that the cold was cutting through my foam parka to my bones.

Uncle Wrexel was seated in his deep, wide chair, which had a special back support built into it. He had gone quite grey but his shoulders were still bony and broad, and he looked as much like his brother, my father, as he always had.

He didn't know me at first. "Why, Roxy," he said, after he had gazed and gazed at me. "Are you on duty?"

"No. I came for the Meeting. How are you?"

"Wonderful! Have you heard about my cucumber?"

"Your cucumber is famous everywhere," I said. He hooked one foot into a flat plastic stool and drew it over near him. I sat down by his knee. He took my chin in his hand and looked hard at me.

"How's that tumbling brother of yours?"

"He's fine. And Mom sends her love."

"Do you want to tell me why you're here? I know it isn't just to see me, though I'm glad you stopped by."

"I came to speak for Vogl. I hope you aren't shocked."

"I haven't been shocked for years," he said, rather dreamily. "Not even by a cucumber with carotene. Well, that's nice. You

108

young people must stick together or the fuddies will eat everything up."

It was hard to tell whether he was becoming senile or whether he meant exactly what he said. There was no particular expression on his face to help me.

"What are you working on now?" I asked.

"Snap beans, my dear. Snap beans which will grow with their roots in bog, at a temperature of one hundred and five degrees."

"For use on Vogl," I said.

"Well, of course. They have to eat, don't they?" There was an open microfilm screen on the desk, and he switched the light off, then swung part way round in his mobile chair. "You don't think snap beans very important," he remarked.

"Food is terribly important," I said. "No food, no people. On the other hand, no people, no need for food."

"Quite so," he said, dreamy again. "I shan't be at the Meeting. I never go. When it's all over, will you come and have dinner with me?"

"If I'm still in one piece, Uncle Wrexel, nothing would please me more."

"Good girl," he said. Then suddenly there was nothing at all senile or dreamy about his sharpness. "One must ask for food, Roxy, but one must never beg for crumbs. It's bad for the stomach. And it's rotten politics!" Then he swung his chair back to the desk, and I could see I was dismissed.

Night had clapped down its lid on this part of the world. I worked my way back into the parka jacket while I stood at the door, looking out at the jitney stop, waiting for the flashing blue light which would indicate a jitney was there. I'd hardly gotten into the parka when the blue light showed. Perhaps they ran more frequently this time of evening.

I went through the inner doors, then through the airsealed

outer lock, and I ran because I didn't like the way the black cold made me feel. The jitney door was opened for me by some kind passenger and I tumbled in. Both my arms were yanked up behind me and a wrist as hard as iron held my throat so tightly I'd have strangled if I tried to speak.

The glass heights of my Uncle Wrexel's domain faded behind us. My hands were secured and my ankles tied tightly before my throat was released. I coughed, and my breath rasped.

"Shut up," somebody said.

The jitney went eerily up and down, soft as a cloud. We passed the dome that housed the hotel and its complex of shops and restaurants. It seemed to me we circled a lot, and then we bored straight at a far dome. An airsealed gateway opened and the jitney plunged in, on through an open-way which slid shut behind us. When we stopped, I was lifted out and carried over a man's shoulder."

"My God," he said, "she weighs a ton. Somebody give me a hand." He took my arms, someone else took my ankles, and they hauled me off like a package down a dimly lit corridor, through a doorway into a well-lighted room, and dumped me on the floor where I was shucked out of my foam parka suit. Half a dozen people were sitting in the room. All of them wore the Vogl trousers that were cut and folded in below the knee. Their skins, of different colors, all had that soft look produced by years of the Vogl climate.

A big man with his hair cut so close his head looked shaven came over and boosted me up to my feet and sort of fed me into a chair. He said, "What a nice piece of luck. A Patrol with a relative in just the right spot. How was your uncle?"

"He's fine, thank you," I said, thinking they hadn't lost a second's time in identifying me and tracking me down.

"How do you think he'd do, dumped out into the snow? He doesn't get around too good, does he?"

110

"I can't see the point of dumping him out into the snow before he's finished up those bog beans for you," I retorted. "I don't see what he has to do with this at all."

"He's just a handle," the big man said. "He's just the handle we hold you by. Now!" He leaned forward from his chair, with an elbow on each knee. "You are a sweet piece of luck. If you didn't happen to bring your uniform along, we can supply you with one. A perfect copy, that is."

"For what?"

Another man, with the big, calloused hands of a farmer, leaned in to our conversation. "For you to stand up at the Meeting and tell them we're right. You've had an inside look. Our kids have to have free access to your planet, and we have to build and staff our own Academies. And most of all, we have to have some decent Universities."

My rage and frustration were so great, I could have cried. "You fools," I shouted. "What do you think I came here for?"

The looks of surprise and suspicion ran like fire around the room. I went on yelling at them. "Did you really think I made such an expensive trip to see my Uncle Wrexel? And you see what you've done? You've ruined it. I won't stand and speak for you now because it'll stink of a setup. Because somebody will find out, and any chance you had of solving this will go right down the drain. I'm so mad I could kill you. You stupid—" My mouth was shut by a knuckled blow from the big man's hand. It split my lip, and blood ran down my chin.

Another voice said, "She means it." The woman who had come in took off her parka and threw it on a chair. I knew her. It was Reba, who had been shipped back to Vogl on probation.

"I know Roxy Rimidon. If she says she came to speak for Vogl, then she means it."

"She'll speak for us," the thin man said grimly.

"Oh, no I won't," I said. "You go right ahead and shoot me on the spot, but I won't say a word for you now."

111

The big man gave a theatrical sigh. "That takes care of Uncle Wrexel. Poor old thing, crawling about on the ice and gasping his last. I bet that synthetic spine pops wide open in the cold. Nasty way to go."

They would do it if they thought it would help their cause. I bluffed, "He's old, and he's been successful. I imagine he's going to die soon anyway."

Another man got up and said, "Come on, we're not getting anywhere this way. I have some much better ideas. Want to put her in the supply closet, or shall we go around to the bar?"

They decided to go around to the bar. My ankles were tied again, and my wrists were firmly attached in back of me to the chair so I could wriggle but not go anywhere. They all went out except Reba, who stalked over and stared at me.

"Were you really going to stick your neck out for us?" she asked. "You know it's very hard to believe."

"I was."

"I'm sorry they cooked it. I *know* you, you'll let them drop your uncle into the snow and you'll let them cut you up in pieces, but you won't do it now, will you? You're so young and stupid and idealistic."

"Thanks," I said.

"They're flatheads," she said. "It was our last resort, to get someone, some public person, to speak up for us." She rubbed her hair with both hands, staring away at the wall. "I don't know what to do now. There's got to be some better way, or at least some way out of this."

"I have an idea," I said.

"I bet you have."

"It would help."

"You expect me to trust you?"

"Have you got a choice?" I asked. "Are you really all out for Vogl, or just for yourself like the others? This is the second time you've been in on a really bad deal."

112

"Softhearted Reba," she sneered at herself. "What else could I do? And they aren't all selfish. They want as much for Vogl as I do."

"I've got an idea," I repeated.

She went across the room and picked her parka up. "Yes, I'll bet," she said, throwing the parka over her shoulders. "Something really great that'll get us all life on a bog farm."

"Not more than two years," I said rashly.

"You! Okay, what is this great idea of yours?"

"Cut me loose. Get me into a jitney and over to Council Headquarters. We'll go in there together and tell them just what happened, how I came on my own to speak for Vogl, and some of you thought it would be a good idea to put pressure on me. That way, I can still get up and speak, on my own."

"You're crazy, Patty. You're quite crazy. You want me to walk into that lion's den? And how can you prove you came on your own, that you aren't just acting because of the pressure we put on?"

"My mother knows why I came."

"Your mother!" She gave a whoop of derisive laughter and disappeared out the door, which hissed shut behind her. A moment later, the lights went out. Evidently they thought I might have second thoughts if I had to sit by myself in the dark.

In a short time I discovered the lights weren't the only thing turned off. It was getting cold. My parka suit was on the other side of the room. If there had been any light I could have seen my breath. Well, freezing to death wasn't as bad as being chopped up.

About the time the cold began to hurt me, making me ache all over, and just before a nice numbness could come and relieve me, the air very slowly began to warm. Were they going to alternately thaw and freeze me until I gave up?

As warm as the air finally became, the warmth still didn't come back to my hands. They must have turned dark blue; my feet didn't feel too wonderful, either. The dark remained. Except for my hands and feet, I grew quite comfortable, and even rather sleepy. I was nodding off into a doze when I realized how cool the air was getting. Right enough, they were going to give me a good dose of climate, on and off, until I hollered for mercy.

I heard the door open. The person came very softly across the room and bent over me. Expecting a blow, I drew back in the chair.

"You promise me only two years?" Reba whispered.

"I can't promise you that. I'm very likely to get a few years on a prison farm myself."

"You knew that when you came. You risked that because you knew we were right."

"That's no help now."

She was quiet for a moment, and then I could feel her working my bonds loose. She said, "That bunch is crazier than I thought. They're even talking about puncturing the dome wall during Meeting. I think if you speak on your own, it'll do a hundred times more good than anything they cook up. And if you risked it, I can. Can you stand up?"

I could stand, but I couldn't use my hands at all. She had to dress me in the foam parka, handling me like a baby. We were trying hard to be quiet. I did my best not to shuffle but she kept whispering, "Sh, sh, can't you pick up your feet, you ox?" Then she had me by one arm, leading me from the room.

The corridor was the longest I ever walked down, but as we went, me shuffling and Reba shushing me, the feeling slowly came back to my feet and the ends of my fingers tingled fiercely with returning life. The open-way door was noisy as it rose. We fled through it and ran toward the jitney which stood just inside the lock.

"Where is it?" Reba muttered frantically, seeking the panel button that would open the air lock. I got into the jitney, next to the driver's seat, and waited for her. There was the hiss of the sealed door opening, and Reba tumbled in beside me and got the jitney going fast. So fast, in fact, that we nearly turned over as we hit the snow.

Reba asked, "Is your mother somebody? Would Council take her word about you?"

"I don't know. She's head of the Bone Bank in her area, but I don't know if they'd take her word, and I would hate to involve her."

"Look, Patty, I don't care who you involve, but make it good and make sure they believe you. It's my neck now, too."

"Glad I didn't throttle it the last time we met," I said.

"I'd like to see you try. I've had as much training as you have, and when we open our first Academy I intend to be at the top."

"Then decontaminate your temper," I said. "You'd be surprised how aggravating a class of rookies can be."

We came to the regular jitney stop in front of Council Headquarters and got out. We stampeded up the path and through the two sets of doors. A Councilman on guard there demanded our identity discs.

"Officer Roxy Rimidon, Planet Patrol, and Reba Smith"— she poked me in outrage at that one—"Vogl Youth Council."

"Never heard of the Youth Council," he said. "Who do you want to see?"

"Who's Dominion Coordinator for this Meeting?"

"You're kidding," he said. "At this time of the night?"

"It's a serious emergency," Reba said quietly.

He turned to the communicator and put through a call. There was a video screen but it remained blank, although from the transmitter came a voice I could swear I knew. "What do you want, Councilman?"

"Two women here, sir. One says she's Planet Patrol. They say it's an emergency."

"Check for weapons and send them up."

115

We got out of our foam suits. He took one look at me and demanded, "Where's your uniform?"

"In my hotel room." I gave him the number so he could check it out if he wanted to.

"Okay, go on up. Take the escalator to the third floor, turn right, it's the gold rosette door."

As we stood on the escalator Reba muttered, "I wish I hadn't done this. I know I'm in for trouble. I feel it in my bones. I wish I hadn't done this."

"But you are going to do it," I said.

"What makes you think so?"

"Because I know you as well as you know me."

We came to the door with the gold rosette on it and paused to look at each other. "You aren't going to back out now," I said angrily.

"No, and neither are you, Patty."

We were told to come in. Tall, powerful, stern, there stood Gen. Marion Bistrup. There was no smile on the face of that tiger.

Reba said, "Good evening, sir. We're sorry to bother you."

"If you're going to waste my time being sorry, then get out," he said. "Which of you pretends to be a Patrolwoman?"

I took a step toward him. "Officer Roxy Rimidon, sir. How's that new kneecap?"

He gaped. Then he shut his mouth with an audible snap. "None of your impertinent damn business," he said. "However, I'll accept your identification for the moment. What is it?"

Nobody sat down. He stood at ease, if you could call that iron stance easy, and we stood stiffly in front of him. Reba collected herself and in a quiet voice began to tell him the story. He never moved a muscle or raised his eyes to her face until she had told him of how I had come to Interdominion North to speak at the Meeting.

Then he looked at me and asked, "Is this true?"

116

"Yes, sir. I felt I must speak. I feel it's important."

"You have a right to speak at an Interdominion Meeting, no matter what you say. But don't expect sympathy. You are a member of the Planet Patrol and it is your duty to maintain our laws. You were trained for it at public expense. If you wish to be associated with the Insurrectionists, some of whom have committed murder and most of whom have loudly cried out for the overthrow of the existing order, then you will get exactly what you deserve. You can expect no mercy."

"I didn't come for mercy. I came to speak for something I believe in."

He snorted. "Get out of here, both of you. I hope not to see either of you again, but I suppose I'll be seeing Rimidon in all her infantile glory on the floor of the Meeting. Personally, I think we should be more strict about who is allowed to speak."

"Sir, you can't mean that," I said in a soft and swooning voice. "You are the torch which lights the way for all those who believe in our way of life. I may not agree with you, sir, but I certainly respect—"

"Crap!" he roared. "You traitor, don't you come in here and butter me up. Get out of my sight!"

"Yes, sir," I said, backing off. "Can we protect Reba Smith, who has disassociated herself from those gangsters, to help us to do this the honorable way?"

He stared at me, incredulous and furious. "Are you asking me for amnesty?"

"Not for myself. But she came willingly, knowing that she runs the risk of a long prison sentence. If she's not protected, they'll murder her."

"Damn you," the General said. "You silly, stupid kids, messing about in serious affairs. You're nothing but a pack of idiots." He went over the the communicator and put through a call. "Fix up something for two females. Get them beds somewhere. Somewhere where they can't get out, or get at the young men, or into trouble. If it's got bars or an electric door that's all the better. Get up here on the double and take them away."

When he'd finished that, he looked over at me again. "Did you bring a uniform or were you going to sneak in as a private citizen?"

"My uniform is at the hotel."

"Very good. That way, you can bring total disgrace to the whole Patrol instead of just to yourself." A very peculiar expression crossed his angry face for an instant. "Not to mention your family. You come from a decent family, and I regret that your actions must inevitably reflect on them."

"You know my mother disagrees heartily with me," I retorted, "and nothing I do or say will reflect badly on her. I speak on my own, sir, and you know it."

A Councilman came in, and General Bistrup ordered, "Remove these two."

We were promptly removed—down, down, into the depths of the dome building. We were locked into an austere room which had two cots, a toilet, basin, and no windows. "Better than the cold, cold grave," I said cheerfully.

"Did you have to be so rude to him?"

"He was casting aspersions on my mother."

"He did it on purpose."

"I know he did it on purpose."

"With your big mouth, I don't see how you've lasted this long in Patrol. You're done for now, aren't you?"

"Right. Done for. Have to go fish farming, I guess. I always wanted to, anyway."

"Cold, cold grave," she said reflectively, sitting on a cot and working her boots off. "You know, on Vogl if we aren't careful where we bury people the underground ferments and bubbles them up, an arm or a leg at a time."

I almost fell for it. When I laughed, Reba said, "While you're out on the floor having a good time tomorrow, what do you think will be happening to me?"

"I think you'll be sitting with the other auditors, hanging onto my every word. Reba, now that we've done this, why don't we stop mean-mouthing each other and act like friends?"

"Don't butter me up," she said.

"I'm not buttering you, you bog balloon. I'm serious."

She unbuttoned her shirt and threw it across the end of the cot. "It would be nice to believe you. But I don't."

"Sweet dreams," I said.

The light remained on in the little room so we pulled our single blankets up over our ears and eyes. But after a minute, I pulled the blanket off my face and said, "Reba, why did you get mixed up with those people a second time?"

"Because I'm stupid," she said.

"No, you're not. You're as smart as they come. I really would like to know."

"How can you know? You've never been in my position. And there are plenty more like me. We used to try speaking out, and writing communiques, and all the proper methods. Nothing at all happened. It was like whistling in deep space."

I wasn't sure of her analogy, but the frustration was clear. In a thin voice she added, "You wait, Roxy. I've got a feeling that one day you'll know just the position I'm in."

"Were you ever charged with any offense?"

"No, I was just on probation after that little caper when we met. What are you doing now, calling in an obligation?"

She was beginning to get under my skin, and rather than get into a real quarrel with her I pulled the blanket up over my head.

In the morning we were both awake when a Councilman unlocked our door and came in with my uniform. He handed it

119

to me and went out without a word. "On an empty stomach," I complained. "They might at least bring us breakfast."

Reba watched me as I dressed. When I tucked the pantaloons into the tops of my boots, she said, "Our uniforms are just like that, only green, and we wear wetboots, of course."

"You mean you even have your uniforms designed?"

"We're full of dreams," she said sadly.

A few minutes later we were led away, but to our pleasant surprise we were taken to a mess hall. They isolated us in a corner, but there was plenty of food and we devoured it ravenously.

A plastic replica of Uncle Wrexel's yellow cucumber was displayed on the wall. I said to Reba, "I'm glad he's okay and your friends didn't have a chance to hurt him. He hasn't quite worked out your bog beans yet, but he will, given a chance."

"You really come from a dazzling family," Reba said. "Here comes our jailie."

The Councilman led us out. We were given our foam suits, we dressed, and were taken to a jitney. It was all very formal, and silent.

The Interdominion Meeting was held in a dome of its own. The center contained a huge auditorium with audio and video stations built in around the walls. Not a word was said in there, not a gesture was made, that was not broadcast for everyone to hear, see, and discuss. It was the working heart that circulated blood through the ten Dominions of Earth and the colony planets of Alpha and Vogl. The left hand knew what the right hand did; the foot did not move without the knowledge of the rib; the lungs did not breathe without the cooperation of the whole body.

Neither of us had ever been present in person at a Meeting. Reba found her way upstairs to the auditors' seats while I was politely shown to a seat in the speakers' section. Mine was the only Patrol uniform in the place. I sat with my boots pulled in under me, feeling as if my cap weighed fifty pounds on my head.

The Councilmen and Dominion presidents came in and took their seats in a semicircle facing us. General Bistrup and several other high-ranking Patrol officers came in last and took their seats. The recording machinery began to give off a hum of business and the Meeting began.

There was no formality except that no rude interruptions were allowed. Some of the speakers were abstract in the extreme; others came immediately to a definite point. The matter of Vogl discontent was discussed at length and in every tone, from hot to cold.

Several presidents felt it was time changes were made; all of these men and women spoke out for more student exchange and for another real University on Vogl. The president of this Meeting, from Africa Dominion, turned and asked if anyone wanted to speak for the public.

I got up. My uniform was noted and a murmur went through the auditorium. "Representatives," I began.

There was the ear-splitting high shriek of Vogl triumph from one of the gallery seats; another murmur and some laughter ran through the crowd. Thank you, Reba, I thought. Then I started to shake. I'd been all right until she encouraged me.

"Representatives," I said again, "I have no sympathy for the groups who try to bludgeon us into action, but I speak for those who want the action and feel no one cares, or listens."

"Do you speak as a Patrol member?" one Councilman asked.

"Yes, sir, I must. I am a Patrol member and not a private citizen."

"Have you been in action against some of the Vogl extremists?" another one asked.

"Yes sir."

"We know who she is," General Bistrup said. "Let her say what she wants."

The first Councilman interrupted again: "I'm curious to know how a Planet Patrol member comes to speak for the very same revolutionary forces she has been trained to control."

"If you let her speak, we may find out," another one said.

There was silence, and I went on. "The Vogl claim to need Patrol Academies of their own is valid. They know their own planet, the physical conditions under which all Vogls must live, and they have plenty of active, intelligent young people ready to be trained for that purpose. I speak for the immediate establishment of one or more Planet Patrol Academies on Vogl. It should be staffed by Earth Patrol instructors until enough Vogls have learned our training methods to staff their own Academies, and that shouldn't take more than two years. I think that freighter space must be found to ship such a teaching staff, with its full equipment, to Vogl, and I think the freighter space would be better used for this purpose, right now, than for shipments of hybrid chicken eggs or bog beans."

Councilmen and presidents began to talk to each other, hot and cold, loud and soft. I was left standing there, wondering how much of the Earth public was with me, or if any portion was. I felt very much alone.

The Scandia Dominion Councilman who had spoken to me first, asked, "Officer, as a fully trained member of Planet Patrol, do you think the Vogls are ready for their own Academies?"

"It's past time for them, sir. And we have enough to do at home. It would take a burden off our own Patrol members if we weren't always being shipped out to clean up trouble on some other planet." That was stretching it a bit, since most of us would give our eyeteeth for off-planet duty.

More discussion. The Meeting president, in a kind of afterthought, turned his face toward me and said, "If you've finished speaking, you might as well sit down."

I was grateful to collapse in my seat. Most of what I planned to say had gone out of my head. I wondered if my mother had the Meeting tuned in. Probably too busy putting in some ribs or ordering another quart of marrow or, considering the time difference, having dinner with Jack Santiago, that charming but terrible bore. I didn't think he was so bad. I thought my mother would be happy with him and I'd be glad to have him in the family.

"The Meeting is recessed until after lunch," the president said. Everyone got up and began moving out. While I was looking around for my jailer, someone tapped me on the back. A Councilman was standing there. "Come along, Officer. General Bistrup wants to talk with you."

There goes my head, I thought. I glanced back into the gallery where Reba was standing with our jailer at her side. She raised her palm outward in the ancient pantomime of friendship. Then she was taken away.

I followed the Councilman around in back of the semicircle of seats, out an exit door, and down another of those corridors where every sound was magnified and echoed as if we were in the bowels of the Earth. I was shown into a room where General Bistrup and several Councilmen were already seated. A blue Patrol dossier lay on a table. I was sure it was mine.

Before anyone got a chance to speak, General Bistrup said, "I want you to know that I disapprove. I think we are far too hasty. I do not think the word or opinion of a junior female Patrol member should influence Council presidents."

"Now, Marion," the Scandia Dominion Councilman said. "You've already been outvoted."

That made me curious, for no voting had yet taken place.

"I don't have to like it," the General replied, "but as long as I'm in uniform, I'll say what I think is the truth."

That was one of those weird statements which now and then struck my sensitivity as both grotesque and hilarious. Though I supposed it was a good thing he had the uniform on, and thus was forced to speak his truth.

They seated me formally in a large chair. A thoughtful silence fell. It was cruel and unusual treatment, as far as I was concerned.

One of the Councilmen finally said, "Officer, it's just as well that you spoke today, though you jumped us."

Without moving my head, I shifted my eyes to him. He was looking at me with interest and curiosity. He went on, "We had already decided some time ago that we'd establish an Academy on Vogl this year. And the first shipment of educational computer components for their new University has already gone out. The news was not to be made public until later."

Then I, and Reba, had gone to the chopping block for nothing. So much for the myth that all decisions were arrived at during public meetings. I was young and stupid, gullible and idealistic.

"As Councilman David said," another voice came in, "we're glad you did speak. It gives us a voice from the public to help us."

Were they going to pin roses on me? I opened my mouth to protest, but someone said, "Be quiet, Officer."

General Bistrup looked me coldly in the eyes. "I disapprove, but I must comply. At least we'll be able to keep an eye on you, Rimidon." He turned to the others and just tossed it off. "It's time she met her superior officer for her next assignment."

They opened the door and in came a Corporal. She was slim and wiry, with one blue eye and one brown. Her blue Patrol uniform had been adapted to Vogl, with the pantaloons cut in under the knee and folded into shiny black wetboots. Her cap sat at a rakish angle on her black curls. Corp. Merle Doucette acknowledged my presence with a raised eyebrow, and politely inclined her head to the gathering.

General Bistrup asked, "Corporal, are you sure Rimidon won't be too sympathetic toward the wrong people?"

"I'm sure, sir. She has a good record and a cool head."

That seemed to be all there was to it, for the Councilmen quietly got up and departed. Merle said to me, "I'll see you in Room thirty-eight for briefing in half an hour, Rimidon."

"Yes, ma'am," I said. She nearly winked at me, but not quite.

Behind me, General Bistrup said, "Officer, you just stay here for a moment. I want to speak with you."

I stood there until the room emptied, then swung around and said, "Sir, what about Reba? Can she be returned to Vogl? She'd make a first-class Planet Patrol."

"You discuss that with Corporal Doucette," he said heavily. There was a video on the table and he set the controls. When the screen lighted, he began putting through a private call, referring to a note to get the series of numbers correct. Then he beckoned me over to the table. I stood just close enough to see my mother's face appear on the screen.

She opened her reception line and smiled out. "Hello, darling," she said. It took me a full moment to realize she couldn't see me where I was standing, and that the darling was not me at all.

I stifled an exclamation. General Bistrup took me by the arm—not roughly but with no gentleness, either—and drew me into my mother's line of vision. "Oh, hello, *darling*," my mother said.

I looked up at his face. He avoided my look and spoke to Mom. "Here she is, Mahiri. We're shipping her out to Vogl as fast as possible. Just as we always have done with trouble-makers."

"Oh, I'm so glad she got the assignment," Mom said. Her eyes focused on me. "I wasn't sure they'd select you, but I did know Merle was heading up the staff and how pleased you'd be to work with her. Good luck, Roxy."

General Bistrup said, "Mahiri, which of us should tell her?"

"You don't need to, either of you," I said. "I don't approve, but I will comply."

125

"Don't pull that on me," he roared. "Just because I marry your mother doesn't mean you get a single special privilege."

"No, sir, it doesn't," I agreed. I turned back to the screen and said to Mom, "I'll see you when we come back."

"Good-bye, darling. And don't be too antagonistic toward the other point of view. I always thought you too liberal, myself."

"Good-bye," I said to both of them, and went out.

◆

Merle was in a lounge with a young lieutenant named Riker Paisley and an older man, Capt. Ben Slane. He had a round face and almost no eyebrows, which gave him a pompous look. But when he smiled it was with friendly warmth. After we were introduced, Merle added, "You three are the advance staff. You'll go on ahead to set up Academy classes and I'll join you a little later. Right now, we've got two weeks of hard work and planning before you get into space."

I blurted, "Wait a minute. I have a friend from Vogl who's going to be a lot of help to us."

Merle said, "Is she around here?"

"She's in lockup. Can you get her out?"

She got on the communicator and ordered, "Release that Vogl woman and make her comfortable until this evening."

"Merle," I said.

"What now, Roxy?"

"How long have you known about the Vogl Academy?"

The others looked bored. Merle said, "A week, maybe two."

"I always thought these things were decided at the Inter-dominion Meetings."

"They are, aren't they? You heard them discussing it this morning, and you got up and spoke."

"But—"

"Oh, grow up, Roxy."

126

We might be working in a system that was the best yet, but it sure wasn't good enough. Not yet.

"I'm growing," I said, but Captain Slane was too busy discussing our orders to hear me, and the others were too busy listening to him.

A hard blow on my forehead brought me up from deep sleep to astonished wakefulness. Instead of playing possum to find out who was doing me in, I raised my head abruptly and received a second blow, which caused me to slide sideways out of the bunk to the cold metal floor. Then I lay there cursing my stupidity, cursing the freighter, cursing my assignment to Vogl, and most of all my idiocy in mistaking the bulkhead for an attacker.

The door of the tiny cabin opened. Even in silhouette I recognized Lt. Riker Paisley, a lean man with a face both sad and humorous—sad eyes, humor lines at eye corners and around the mouth. I lay there in the light that streamed in and wondered whether, to complete the picture, I should weep.

"What are you doing?" Rike inquired in a mild voice.

I raised myself on one elbow, aware of the bruising blows I'd received from the bulkhead in my restless sleep. "Oh, I'm just lying here thinking things over," I said.

He touched on the light and came near me. He had no boots,

128

just socks pulled up over his bony ankles and his uniform trousers flopping loose above the socks. His shirt was unbuttoned over his hairy chest. "What are you doing, Officer?" he repeated.

I sat up and looked at his feet.

"Bunk too small?" he asked. "Roll off, did you?"

"That's just what happened, but I'm ashamed to admit it."

He laughed and gave me a lift to my feet. "Roxy, I've already done the same thing twice. Go back to sleep."

He touched off the light and went out. I climbed back into the bunk and pulled the allcover up over my ears. The crew was sullen, the food terrible, and we were getting nervous and fidgety as the trip lengthened out toward Vogl. All of us except Reba. She was glad to be going home and kept promising to show us the sights, including the fermenting cemeteries.

The ship was loaded with cargo, most of it hybrid grains which would probably rot in Vogl's squashy soil before they germinated. The passenger quarters were little more than closets, with a metal bunk shelf covered with foam plat. Crew, passengers, officers—all got the same accommodations. The galley was a joke: two infraboxes, a bottomless supply of krilbits, and a faucet I'd never been allowed to touch. Capt. Ben Slane swore that you could get oil from the faucet for a robot crew, since no human crew could be induced to take the trip twice.

At breakfast the third day out Ben had raised his almost invisible eyebrows and muttered, "Stuff your krilbits."

"Sure," Cookie had replied obligingly, and at lunch we were served tough little pastry pouches stuffed with more krilbits. Such were the luxuries of the *Sun Dial*.

Rike wondered, "What do they do with Important People on these trips?"

Ben said, "Tank them, of course."

Although life-immersion tanks were still in the research

stage the subject was likely to come up on these trips. Meanwhile, the only help for those who wanted it was a slowdown drug. As we were supposed to be spending the time discussing the problems of setting up a Vogl Patrol Academy, we were perfectly clear-headed and free to complain about the conditions. We spent a lot of time playing chess and I got to know and like Riker Paisley. Sometimes we'd just communicate with our eyes: I like you. I looked forward to working with him. In fact, I looked forward to working.

At one breakfast Reba said cheerily, "Wait until you taste tilapia chowder."

"I can't wait," Ben said. "Do you have any beer?"

Mock scandalized, Reba demanded, "You mean on board?"

"He means do you make your own on Vogl," Rike said, spooning up the puddinglike breakfast food.

"We make everything we need," Reba said darkly.

"You are going out in the field with me, aren't you?" I asked.

"I wouldn't dare let you go alone. On those rare occasions when we get a Patty in the field, there is nothing but grief. I told you before, the first thing they do is fall into a bog, or collapse from the heat, or meet up with some indigenous life form and get a head nipped off."

"Has that ever really happened?" I asked, though of course I'd heard about Vogl reptiles before.

"It only happened once, the first time a Patrol group came. We talked about having the Sergeant's headless body stuffed and put in our museum but decided against it."

"Pity," I said.

"Stop worrying. Those big reptiles are as dumb as they come and they're not aggressive. They only bite if you get between them and their food."

This was about the only real information we could pry out of Reba. She refused to answer questions of practical value, saying we'd have to form our own impressions and she didn't

130

want to influence us. Several times she referred to what she called "local problems" but wouldn't identify them. She just said, "Oh, you'll become familiar with them in no time." Confined as the four of us were in such small quarters for eight days, her attitude did nothing to make us happy and relaxed.

During the last dinner before touchdown, Reba said, "Wait'll you see Bluebeard's Castle." But by this time no one would rise to her bait anymore, and we just glowered at her over our hulled wheat and kril fritters.

The spaceport was on a high plateau west of the major body of water, Azure Ocean. Azure it was, close to the overgrown green shore; farther out it darkened to cobalt. It was rich with life, both nutritious and poisonous.

When we docked a group of dark, stocky men were loading freight onto another ship, readying it for takeoff. The ground was hard but crunchy, composed of millions of broken shells. The buildings were long, flat structures with permaflex screening and huge roof drains to carry off the gallons of water from the frequent storms. Behind the port, the mountains were a dark, vivid green. One faintly smoking cone told of recent volcanic activity. The air was hot, wet, and smelly, though we passed through zones of sluggishly moving air which smelled very sweet.

We were all struck by the quiet and the miles and miles of dense green growth. Across the ocean, distances were pale blue stained with lavender. And beyond that, far to the south, lay another land mass with its own capital town of Bragby. That was where the new University was being set up.

We passed the packing houses where Vogl's perishable foodstuffs were cryotransferred before shipment. One building was labeled MEDICAL. I asked Reba about it.

"That's where organs and tissue are stored. We never ship any out; there's a lot more demand for them on a recently settled planet than you could imagine at home."

We reached the shell flats where half a dozen small helicars were parked and got into one. Reba was at the controls. She said, "When we pass over Gill Glade, we may find some kids having a ceremony there. I'd like to stop so you can see it."

"What kind of ceremony?" Ben asked.

"A disapproved one, I can assure you. We have a group of people who call themselves Dust Bowlers."

Rike snorted. "They'll have to go some to find dust around here. What is it, some kind of religion?"

Reba set the helicar in motion and we rose above the port. "It's both religious and political. We used to think they were harmless-crazy, but we turned out to be wrong. You'll see."

Once in the air, everything below showed solid green. There was no sign of a port, a town, a glade, or an opening. It didn't look as if there were a single place in this world to put a helicar down. We were flying parallel to a great mountain range; puffs of dark smoke rose occasionally from Mt. Kesthar, which was still active. Down toward the equatorial line stood more bare volcanic peaks, which still erupted, and miles of lava beds, but both the port and northern capital of Davvis were well above the major quake and eruption zones.

"We get occasional tremors," Reba explained.

The helicar began to swoop downwards. We couldn't see anything, but evidently Reba did. "Gill Glade," she said. "They usually come out around noon. They don't mind spectators as long as no one interferes or shows any signs of disapproval. But you must keep quiet. If you think they respect your blue uniforms, you're wrong."

The helicar went on down toward what appeared to be solid growth. I could see Rike gritting his teeth in anticipation of a crash. First a band of paler green appeared, then a band of lettuce-yellow opened up. Whether it was cleared or a natural opening, we couldn't tell, but we could see some figures in a circle. Reba brought the helicar down at one end of the glade and we got out, careful to be quiet. None of the people so much as glanced at us.

"I put the fat bowl down," the tall man said, and did so, in the center of the glade.

"He puts the fat bowl down," the people said.

"I put the three stems down," the small girl said.

"She puts the three stems down," said the people.

"I put down the dust," said the tall man.

"I put down the shadow of dust," said the small girl.

"They put down the dust, they put down the shadow of dust, they put down that which dries up the wet, that which holds back the cloud, that which shapes the land firm," the people said.

It was the mindless expression on the faces that I found scary. We stood at the end of the glade and watched them perform what looked like primitive god-magic. In itself, it was harmless, a form of entertainment or release. But the people taking part in it looked severe and withdrawn. They weren't having fun or giving thanks, they were working desperately hard at something they felt desperately serious about. If too many young Vogl citizens participated in this kind of thing, putting bowls on the ground and chanting about dust, they'd never come to grips with a practical means of making the wet, boggy planet habitable.

When I whispered this thought to Reba, she said, "That's it. That's exactly it. They've turned against any kind of technology, even against the hybrid animals and foods which keep us alive. They say they're unholy. They want the planet left just as it was found, claiming they can live off it their own way."

The tall man chanted, "Dust of man, dust of God, dust of ashes," and sprinkled some dust around the bowl. The group made similar sprinkling motions, though they held nothing but air in their fingers. "Dust," they murmured. "Dust!" they sang. "DUST!" they cried, sprinkling the invisible particles.

133

The ceremony seemed to be winding down on this monoto-
nous note and we silently crowded back into the helicar for the
rest of the journey. We passed over miles of green, patches and
splotches of blue, ponds and small lakes, then more quaking
pale green of bogs, mountains, hills, all green, green, green. It
made my eyes ache.

◆

Davvis had a mayor named Jimmy Kim, a theater, a ball field
of broken shell packed hard (something to keep your face off
when you slide home), and the General Hospital. On the
outskirts of Davvis, to the north, built up high above bog pools,
was the Vogl School of Agriculture.

To east and west spread the hard-worked terrace farms, each
with its freshwater pool of tilapia fish. One pair of tilapia
was dried, to boost the protein value. Hairless hybrid goats
were the only other source of animal protein, although a certain
fungus diseases, and would breed in fresh or brackish water.
Best of all, they subsisted very well on such waste matter as
cereal hulls, cut grasses, and leaves. The tilapia were everybody's dream food. The could be ground into a tasteless,
odorless meal which might even be added to spaghetti before it
was dried, to boost the protein value. Hairless hybrid goats
were the only other source of animal protein, although a certain
variety of rabbit was being tested.

On the higher terraces new kinds of rice were being grown.
Topmost, behind the bungalow homes built above the worked
terraces, stood groves of fruit trees. The shrubby, blue-leaved
ones were reems.

"Our very own," Reba said. "Wait'll you taste them."

"I have," I reminded her.

As we came to the center of town we could see that everyone
was on foot except the delivery people. They drove loaded
electric carts along a central raised mall. There was a big,

impressive building at one side of the main square. I thought it must be the Mayor's house.

"Bluebeard's Castle," Reba announced.

"Not likely," Ben said. "What is it, really?"

On second look, it had that institutional appearance you can recognize anywhere. A formal border of shrubs lay on each side of the walk going up to the broad steps. Under one of the shrubs lay some unusual object. It was completely smooth, shiny even in the shade. It looked as if it were made of metal. Reba gave a soft but distinctive whistle. The machinery got up on four unjointed legs and trotted toward us. The hair rose on the nape of my neck. Its skull was streamlined and earless, with what looked like small vents but couldn't be nostrils. It had no tail.

"Hello, Cy," Reba said to it. It had stopped about six feet from us and we could see it had eyes, of the TV camera type.

Rike sucked in his breath sharply. "What is it?"

"A cydog," Reba said. "There's always one on guard here. I told you, this is Bluebeard's Castle."

"Now just a minute," Ben said, sounding his most pompous. "Is there any part of that thing which is real dog?"

"The brain is real dog, Captain," Reba said. Obviously she was enjoying this encounter with her own kind of bitter glee. "The brain is sixteen generations purebred guard dog. The body was discarded after we imported the stock. We discovered there isn't any breed of dependable guard dog which can work in this climate, let alone sit outside on twenty-four-hour duty and communicate with those inside. All Cy needs is a little recharge now and then and a special solution to keep its brain moist."

Ben asked, "Has it got teeth?"

"It doesn't need teeth. It carries an anesthetic needle. We fondly call it a fang." Reba turned away, the cydog went back to the shade of the shrubs, and we moved on.

"Why do you need a guard there?" I asked.

Reba shook her head. "Just in case some of those Dust Bowlers come to town, or an Earth Patty gets too nosy, or something like that."

Sweating, thirsty, and stunned by the heaviness of the overheated air we went through town toward the hotel where we'd have to stay until the Academy building was completed. Rike finally asked the question for all of us: What was inside the Castle?

"Medical Research," Reba said. "Here's your hotel."

The cooling units were going full blast. The relief was tremendous. We sat together sipping cool fruit drinks in the lounge, which was dim and low-roofed. Its walls were of the lovely porous fanwood used in most of the Vogl buildings. Suddenly, in the space between two breaths, it grew darker and darker, the lobby lights came on, and sheets of rain fell. We sat and watched it pour, wishing it were tomorrow, wishing we could finally get down to work.

Although neither the sleeping quarters nor the roof drains had been completed in the Academy building we went over there in the morning and started setting up classrooms around the computer nest. Reba, in her green Vogl Patrol uniform with its fishnet tunic, arrived early. I deputized her as my field adjutant, which was a laugh. She had all the field knowledge; I didn't even own a pair of bog shoes. Reba was cheerful today; perhaps, like the rest of us, she was relieved to be put to work.

"Got something for you," she said, "a little present from some of us on Vogl . . . for what you did at the Meeting." She put the gift on my table, where it hesitated for an instant, then its tiny wheels turned and it ran up my arm onto my shoulder. It was a metal mouse.

"You don't really expect me to believe there's a mouse brain inside this mechanical device?" I asked.

"Sure. There are only two of them, though. Dr. Mensy gave mice a whirl when she was on vacation. She claims they aren't good for anything but amusement."

I plucked it off my shoulder. Dr. Mensy must be a whimsical vacationer. She had given it mousy metal ears and one little eye in the middle of its nose. It also had a neck joint, which permitted it to cock its head in an appealing way. I sort of liked it. "Do I oil it?" I asked.

"Cyborgs aren't my field. Dr. Mensy can tell you, and you'll meet her soon. Meanwhile, are you aware that Academy applicants are lined up in the hall about six deep?"

"Just a minute, Reba. This is an agricultural planet and there's been a lot of trouble between Vogl and Earth because you wanted a major University and a chance to do more than grow goats and beans. Now here is this mouse, and there was that dog thing, and yet we still haven't produced working cyborgs on Earth. Would you like to explain how all this happened on Vogl?"

"Roxy, you're like all the rest of them. You don't listen when we tell you. It's been a long time since many of our young people decided they didn't have to be farmers, that they could be astronomers or genetic engineers or whatever they wanted. We've been smuggling as much equipment off Earth as we can, and what counts more, we've collected the best brains on Vogl right here in Davvis. We have all the know-how here. What did you expect, Patty, a complacent bunch of farmers, sweating out their lives just to feed your planet?"

"But do you know how advanced these techniques are?"

"You bet we do. You've got a thousand different opportunities, and a thousand different directions to go in. Your energies are spread pretty thin. Up here, along with plain old-fashioned survival, we've concentrated on medical en-

137

gineering. We know its value. Now how about setting up the schoolhouse?"

A Dr. Petes had been drafted to serve as Academy medic and had set up an examination center in a storeroom at the end of the hall. The Vogl applicants were a mixed group, all right—all shapes, sizes, colors, and conditions, though thin seemed to be the rule. I wondered whether it was their diet or the climate. I hoped it was the latter.

Before we started interviewing I asked Reba, "Do you think any of those Dust Bowlers would try to sign up to make trouble, or to see what's going on?"

"Not a chance. This is dirty territory, the whole town is. From their point of view the Academy is a wicked place. Besides, Bluebeard's Castle is their ultimate target, the unholy of unholies."

"Are they your 'local problems,' Reba?"

"It would be better if you came to your own conclusions," she said as stuffily as Captain Slane at his worst.

Despite our good intentions we began interviewing amidst mass confusion. Papers turned soggy at a touch and the moist Vogl heat turned our brains to jelly. I admired again the fanwood interiors and furniture, dry but resiliant. I wished I were the same.

The people of Vogl came to peer in curiosity at our work tables and our faces; at least half of them had turned out just for the spectacle. A boy with green eyes and a beautiful smile shambled into the room and announced himself as Ally Stahr. He sprawled on one of the little hard chairs, something that looked impossible to do on such a perch. Practice, I supposed.

"I can milk goats," he said, grinning at us. "And I've designed computer systems, done a little surgery—"

"Surgery?" I croaked.

"Yeah, some," he said. "Lots of us learn to do some, just the basic stuff. I know farms as well as towns and I grew up on bogshoes. I ought to be of some use."

"I play the noseflute," I said, with as much insouciance as I could muster.

"In our climate, the reeds warp," the boy countered mercilessly.

Rike asked, "How old are you?"

"Fifteen and three quarters."

"Underage," I replied.

"Wait, Roxy," Reba said. "This is Vogl. If Ally's got the background and experience we need, then we should use him."

Ben Slane puffed himself up and withheld the nice smile that made him so likeable. "Fifteen, indeed! There have to be some regulations."

I thought it over for about three seconds. "Captain, maybe Reba's right. Don't you think we ought to set up Vogl regulations rather than using our own? We're going to face some unknown situations here, aren't we?" We'd found it was always a good idea to put our thoughts in the form of questions to the Captain. Then he could agree with us while sounding as if he were the final authority.

Slane pulled his chin in toward his neck, and gave the question his profound consideration. "All right. Perhaps we can use him in some capacity. Send him along to Dr. Petes."

We continued screening applicants. What struck me most about all of them—boys, skinny young women, work-hardened older farmers—was a quality of tough realism. It made me feel soft—me, with my training, someone who'd always been proud of physical toughness and mental competence. I felt like a luxury item compared to the average citizen of Vogl. It gave me something to think about, like who was going to teach whom what.

After we'd shut down for the morning Reba sat herself on my desk and began to clean her fingernails. I took Cyclops, my cymouse, out of the table drawer where he'd been put for safety. "Reba, did I thank you for this critter?"

"No, but you're welcome. I think you ought to meet Annie Mensy. She'll be interested in you."

I looked into her eyes, but she met my look with no expression. I was learning that's how Vogl people usually look at you, unless something strikes them as funny. Beware of that laughter, I told myself.

"Why does she want to see me?" I asked. "I'm not ready to be encased in metal."

Reba laughed. "At the level of officer, you don't qualify." She slid off the desk. "Come on. I promised Dr. Mensy I'd bring you over."

"Okay. Where is she?"

"She's at Bluebeard's Castle. She's the queen there."

I followed her in silence. We were crossing the main square before Reba said, "We don't really know that you'll work out, of course."

"How come you know so much? You've been away on Earth for months. I don't know what you're talking about."

"Corporal Doucette had a few words with me. If you want to blame anyone for anything that happens, blame your friend Merle."

The cydog under the shrub merely lifted its head, then went back to rest again, apparently content. The door to Bluebeard's Castle was unlocked and there was no human guard. I began to think I was being had—again.

Inside, the corridor was low-roofed, cool, and dim. At intervals there were opaque panels set into the walls which I was sure transmitted all kinds of information. A door slid open and out came a tiny, dark, fierce-looking woman. "There you are!" she cried, darting up to us. "Roxy Rimidon? Yes, of course. We've been waiting all morning for you."

Feeling edgy and disagreeable about all these mysteries, I sounded nearly as stiff-necked as Ben Slane when I spoke. "It's supposed to be my job to set up some sort of Patrol Academy."

"Yes, sweetheart, I know," Dr. Mensy said, "but we're sure you have other talents. Corporal Doucette sent instructions for us to use you in some experiments. And after all, you've borrowed our Dr. Petes and we can hardly spare him. Of course, darling, I'm not suggesting that we received a fair trade."

"See you later," Reba said, and escaped my clutching hand.

"Do come in, dear," Dr. Mensy said, beckoning me from her doorway. Inside, it was the usual green plastic environment one expects in medical centers, harsh-looking after the beautiful fanwood walls and ceilings.

"Thanks for the cymouse," I said, remembering that Cyclops was in the breast pocket of my blouse. I took him out and looked him in the eye. He cocked his head sideways and looked back smugly at me, so I put him away again.

"Oh, that was the fun one," Annie Mensey said, smiling. "No intelligence, but awfully cute. We don't usually bother with cute things around here. I was ashamed I'd spent time on those." She sat at her desk and went through some papers, then motioned me over to one of the small hard chairs everyone on Vogl seemed to find necessary to their comfort. For a few minutes there was that silence which is composed of quiet noises: ventilators, coolers or heaters, the whispering of stiff, official papers. A voice over her desk speaker said: "Ready? Domingo is about burning off his insulation with impatience."

"No," Dr. Mensy said, not even raising her eyes from her papers. "Tell him to turn off for about ten minutes. Officer Rimidon is in no way prepared."

"Lots of luck," said the voice. A little sweat began to come out on my upper lip. I loved every part of me and didn't intend to give any of it up to these mad surgeons.

Dr. Mensy finally looked up at me. "Well, darling, tell me, do you know anything about adapted man?"

"Only theoretically. You don't mean you've got a metal man walking around?"

Her grin was ferocious, her intensity laserlike. "Look," she said. "A cyborg may or may not be mobile; what it has is amplified brain power, especially our immobile type, which has been extended, or incorporated, into a computer. There are other adaptations in other cases—mechanical, electronic, and so on. You know. If you're out on bogshoes somewhere you don't have access to a computer. But your cyborg partner does."

I swallowed, then I asked, "Whatever happened to the idea of robot doubles?"

"They've been in use here and there, but the robot brain is limited as long as it's portable. Maybe someday it won't be. But let's think about today's work."

"And tomorrow's," I said, standing up. "Thanks, but I decline. I was sent here to teach a Patrol Academy."

"Oh, darling, you couldn't be more mistaken," she said, flinging a set of papers across the desk to me. "Teach later, perhaps," she added. The papers were orders, signed by General Bistrup. I was to cooperate in an experimental medical venture with Dr. Annie Mensy of Medical Research. At the bottom of all this official stuff, there was a note to the effect that if the experiments were successful I was to be in charge of field work.

I sat there thinking about Domingo, who even now was sizzling through his insulation. "Tell me about Domingo, Dr. Mensy."

"His body was crushed in a rock slide and his chances for physical survival were absolute zero. His brain is now tremendously amplified by the link to a computer and he's willing to survive any way he can. So far he is the only human survivor of the applications of our research. We lost the other two to brain damage during the bionic installation phase."

"I see," I said numbly.

Dr. Mensy tapped the speaker on her desk and said, "Tell Domingo we're coming down now."

We went down the corridor to a flight of steps. As we began to descend the steps my skin felt crawly and hot. Right foot down, I said: Why me? Left foot down, I said: Not me! I stopped short, holding onto the grab rails on both sides.

"Listen. I don't think I can be of any use to you, Dr. Mensy."

"Oh, yes, you can," she said, taking me by the arms and pulling me. "At least you can try."

Another shiny green room, this one vast. The far end was given over to a computer installation with a video screen set into its center and a couple of stereo speakers. I had no idea where in that mass of circuits, synapses, and relays somebody named Domingo, or the remains of him, was hiding. Suddenly out of the speakers came: "Wow. Lookit her. A brown-eyed blonde. Hook us up, Doctor."

The voice was not the canned kind I had expected. It sounded extremely real. It even cracked part way through the comments. Dr. Mensy was rolling a padded chair with a crown of metal and wires forward toward Domingo.

"You'll get used to him," she said. "Come and sit down. Domingo, this is Officer Rimidon of Planet Patrol."

"Yeah, hi. I was afraid they'd send me some mean old lady. This is my lucky day."

"Doctor, how old is Domingo?" I asked.

"About thirteen now. He was eleven at the time of his

143

accident. If you're wondering about his voice, we took it off tapes and reprinted it."

"Just a little nicety you thought up on vacation?" I asked, backing away from the chair she was offering me.

"Something like that," she said absently. "Sit down."

So I sat down. She wired me up, working gently. Domingo's assortment of lights, keys, stereos, and screens hummed and blinked. At one point it even sang a few bars of song. Dr. Mensy lowered the metal crown to my head and I thought what a fool I was to walk into this. It was an encephalotransfer machine; they'd take everything they needed out of my head and leave me to bumble around their planet. Or they'd just dispose of me in a bog, along with Ben and Rike, and set up their own Academy. Domingo was nothing but a recording; the computer they tried to pass off as a boy was just a computer. I'd walked right into it and now there was no way out. But I had seen the signed orders.

"Okay, darling, let's begin," Dr. Mensy said just as I was going to reach up and snatch that stuff off my head.

There was a moment of panic. My stomach turned over, and every primeval fear I'd buried since childhood came to the surface writhing and leering. Then I seemed to hurtle down an interminable black funnel while something—a shape, or rather a point of light—hurtled toward me. It struck me full on. To keep myself from falling I grabbed it and found I was holding the thin body of a weeping boy. This is not real, I thought.

"Sure it's real," Domingo thought inside my own head. "It's me. It's you. It's the onliest time since Mrs. Farrel left for Alpha that anybody's been able to touch me."

How can I touch what isn't there? I thought.

"I'm here, Blondie. 'Touch' is in the brain, you know."

Then the physical sensations faded and the darkness lifted

gradually until I could see a light shining on green tile, Dr. Annie Mensy in her green slacks and smock, Domingo's stereo voice boxes, my own arms, furred with soft blonde hair, and my sweating fingers gripping the arms of the chair. Shakily, I reached up to my head, only to find it free of entanglements. Just my own head, my own blonde waves.

"Hi," Domingo's voice said through the stereo. And inside my head it said, "Hi," like an echo.

"Contact?" Dr. Mensy asked.

"Too much," I said. "Now what?"

"Now, bogshoes and out into the field with you. Domingo reads the map and gives you directional signals. You feed back what you see and hear."

"You mean right now? What if we lose contact? I never did anything like this before. I don't know how to do it."

She gave me the no-person look so common on Vogl and said, "Domingo knows how. Mrs. Farrel did, too, but her family transferred to Alpha where surgeons are more scarce than here. Several others have been in contact with Domingo, but they didn't get along too well."

Dr. Mensy took me upstairs, wished me good luck, and sent me out a side door. There, an orderly strapped on a backpack for me, gave me a pair of bogshoes which I slung over my shoulder, and wished me good luck. I walked out toward the dense wall of beeky and fan trees. The growth was incredibly lush. The ground was covered with ferns and creepers and groups of bright, pouched flowers.

"No, go west," Domingo was directing me in my head. "You know which way west is? Curve off to the right. There, that's it." I wished he wasn't so intent on playing tough-and-funny because there was work to do, even if I wasn't sure what it was.

The trees thinned out after a while and ahead of me I could see the pale, quivery green which meant bog. I sat down and strapped on the bogshoes, remembering Lieutenant Nelson at the Academy, who'd taught me how to use them. It seemed a long, long time ago.

I stood up, went forward, flapped and waddled down the squelchy slope to the bog. Half the trick of bogshoes is not slowing down for anything. You have to keep your pace fast and even so that you don't begin to sink. If your feet were circular, about twenty-four inches in diameter, and well webbed, and if you had learned from birth how to balance on these feet, you could cross a Vogl bog fairly well.

I wanted to head up the slope directly in front of me, but Domingo guided me to the right. I cautiously increased my speed as I felt the surface quaking and giving way under me. Slap, slop, slap; wet mud or muddy water, whichever it was, splashed up around me. Legend had it that Vogl children cross bogs in absolute silence, but I knew it had to be a lie.

Among the branches of the trees some beautiful winged lizards glided and crossed overhead, but I couldn't afford more than a glance at them. I was ordered to keep moving.

I'd just made it to the edge of the bog when I stubbed one shoe and over I went—splash, splop—grabbing at solid ground. I managed to drag myself up to safety.

"Clod," Domingo said.

"I'm not used to this," I said in self-defense.

"Yes you are. You're mobile."

"I'm not mobile on bogshoes."

"Clod. Lump. Blonde barge."

"Domingo, we're supposed to work together."

"Stupid. I don't need you. You need me."

He vanished out of my head. I sat there, holding the dripping bogshoes in one hand, with no idea of where I was, where I should go, or how to get back.

So I got up and went forward on the principle that if I'd been sent out in this direction there was somewhere to go.

146

I ended up on one of those open, grassy glades with a group of Dust Bowlers sitting around, evidently finishing one of their ceremonies. I came upon them so suddenly I had no chance to be quiet or careful or even polite; I just tumbled into their midst and kicked over a ritual bowl of dust while I was at it.

They were an extremely hostile-looking group. My Patrol uniform had turned brown with mud and green with slime, but it was recognizable even so.

"Get out of here," one of them said.

"Gladly. Can you show me the way?"

"You mean you're lost?" another one said.

They began to laugh. Then they began to move in a circle around me.

"Domingo!"

"A real-life Patty," someone said.

"Let's put her back in the bog."

"We don't need to, let's just leave her here."

"That's no fun. Let's run her through the woods."

A clump of mud, with some roots attached, struck me on the cheek. One of them said, "She can't interfere with us now, it's far too late."

"Domingo? I need you!"

"That's right," Domingo finally responded. "You need me. What have you got in your pockets?"

Cyclops had ridden out the journey in my blouse pocket. On the off chance that Domingo knew what he was doing, I took Cyclops out and held him in the palm of my hand. The group voiced revulsion, fear, and hate.

"Evil. Corrupt. Stinking. Vile. Unholy." They chanted a long list of these expressions.

Cyclops gleamed in the palm of my hand. In my head Domingo said: "Don't move, partner, just stand there and drip mud." I wasn't sure if that was designed to help me or mock me.

"Why is it evil?" I asked the young woman who seemed to be in charge of the group.

"It isn't human. It isn't Godly."

Whatever they felt about the cymouse and me, they were breaking up as a group. One of them began to collect the ritual bowls from the ground. A couple more had turned and gone away among the trees. Muttering and shuffling, glancing back over their shoulder at Cyclops, the rest began to leave. The young woman looked back and said, "No matter what you do, you're too late to stop us."

"Stop what?"

But of course there was no answer. So I thought: "Domingo, I'd like to get back pretty soon."

"Going to have a hot bath, Officer? A cold drink? A big meal? Going to a ball game? To a dance?"

"Would you rather be dead?" I asked.

He shouted loud enough to crack my head. "I *am* dead, don't you understand? All of me's gone except the brain. But it isn't always enough. Please try to understand."

I did, only too well. I wondered if he knew I could easily cry for him. I just asked, "Which way home, partner?"

I turned around and followed crushed leaves and bent branches as well as I could, but this was the kind of forest where any human mark seemed to vanish almost instantly. My muscles ached from the strange terrain. My head hurt, too, probably not through any fault of Domingo's. I could understand why the others hadn't gotten along with him, though.

Now I had to cross the bog again and go back. The second time was a little better, even though I was tired. It wasn't only the wet heat—listening for Domingo was also a new experience for me. And trying to handle him mentally while I handled myself physically was exhausting.

My vision was badly blurred by the time I broke out of the forest and could look down toward the big building I'd left a few hours before. I felt I could just fall down right here and go to sleep forever. But I did make it. I dumped my bogshoes and the backpack, which I'd never opened, on the step, opened the door, and stalked in, trying to look strong and official. Rike was down at the end of the corridor talking with Dr. Mensy.

"I want to be unhooked from Domingo," I said.

Dr. Mensy pursed her lips. "Difficulties?"

"Insurmountable."

"I don't believe it. Go and have some dinner and come back tomorrow."

"Come on," Rike said, and took my arm.

We sat in the hotel lounge with the lovely magic of tall, cold drinks while I told him as well as I could what the day had been like. I was truly grateful for his sympathy. He listened to all I told him, looking relaxed and humorous as he always did.

"Well, it sounds like a rough day," he said when I finished. "I don't believe I'd care for that linkup with Domingo one bit. But you seem to have handled it very well. Come on now, let's have a good meal." He rose to his feet and pulled me up with him. "They have wonderful roast goat here."

"I'd eat roast anything just now," I admitted as we went off to the dining room together.

◆

In the morning as soon as I arrived at the Academy, I was greeted by Captain Slane. "Morning, Officer. You're supposed to go over to Bluebeard's again today."

I noticed how easily we'd all come to call it Bluebeard's Castle. "Listen, the experiment was a flop and I really don't want to go through it again."

He looked at me in amazement. "Officer Rimidon, I just gave you an order."

"Yes, sir," I said, then spun on my heel and went out. Since

149

we had arrived we'd been slopping along comfortably as friends to the degree that I'd forgotten he was my superior, forgotten I was to take orders. In other words, my brain had begun to rot the moment I set foot on this disgusting planet. I could have stayed home and been killed or maimed in any number of conventional ways, and probably my mother would have received my posthumous citation for bravery, intelligence, and dedication to duty.

"Good morning, ma'am," I said to Dr. Mensy when I got to her office.

"Hello, Officer darling," she said. "I understand that Domingo treated you rudely. He said he was sorry."

"That was very nice of him," I replied.

She glared up along her small nose at me. "Don't take that tone. Did you expect him to behave like a regular little school boy?"

"No, I didn't. But you did say the others were unable to get along with him."

"They were just ordinary undisciplined citizens. I'd hoped for better from someone with your background. I would like to link you up again."

"You mean we're unhooked? It wears off?"

"When we link you with Domingo we try to parallel both brain patterns, at least in some areas. Of course we use Domingo's pattern, rather than yours, as a base. If we were to repeat this parallel patterning daily over a period of time, probably your personality would become subordinate to his. I'm not sure that would be desirable. We're not at liberty to try it, anyhow, especially with Patrol personnel. The contact wears off after five or six hours if it isn't repeated daily. Do you understand?"

"Clearly," I lied.

"Then let's go downstairs and see if we can't work out a little more cooperation between the two of you. Enough to see if this immobile cyborg–mobile field officer team has the value we think it has."

She'd no sooner opened the door to Domingo's room than his speakers shouted: "Hi, Blondie."

He gave a raucous laugh. Dr. Mensy looked distressed. "He's just a child," she said.

"No, he isn't," I protested.

Domingo said, "You tell her. I been trying to tell her for a long time now. She thinks I'm a thirteen-year-old boy."

"Well, if you're not, what are you, inside all that gear?" the doctor asked.

"I'm a highly sophisticated thinking machine and you're gonna hook me up to a highly sophisticated feeling machine and together we're gonna dry up those old Dust Bowlers who want to foul up progress for the rest of us. Besides, they don't believe in me."

"Some speech," I said.

"Yeah, I'm pretty good, huh? Come on, Blondie, sit down in the chair. Hook up and be my feelie."

"Okay. We'll hook up and you be my thinkie."

"Oh, dear Lord," Dr. Mensy exclaimed, "I will never understand the layman's mentality. This isn't some sort of joke."

"Yes, it is," Domingo and I said together. This tone of lightheartedness might be just the right one to take, the right way to keep Domingo working clearly and at his best without emotional interference.

This time I went down through the darkness at moderate speed without the panic; this time Domingo didn't hurl himself weeping into my arms. We shook hands, kissed each other on both cheeks, and were committed to a partnership. Or so I hoped.

"Do those Dust Bowlers have any headquarters?" I thought to Domingo.

"Sure, out on the farms. Cross that bog you fell into yester-

151

day, go northeast two miles, and you'll find them. Get going, clumsy."

"You can call me Roxy."

"Sure, Blondie."

"Roxy."

"Dumbhead."

This time I made it across the bog without falling. The glade was empty; only a small pile of nearly vanished dust showed where the group had met before. I followed Domingo's guidance and walked through the forest for a long time until I came to an area where small farms showed in the open distance.

The houses were built on stilts to keep them from fungus and rot. Each had its own vegetable patch, some goats tethered out to graze, and the tilapia pools which seemed to be communally operated.

Otherwise, the place was deserted. The heat was terrific, and my feet were shaking. No, they weren't—the ground was.

I was hurrying up the slope toward the stilt houses when a real tremor occurred. I stopped and looked back. Down by the bog a black mouth opened, grinned, and closed.

"Domingo!"

"Oh, just sit down and wait a bit. We have these little quakes all the time. If you're on high ground you're okay. I can see the place is empty. Maybe they're having a mass ceremony somewhere. Why don't you sit there and look around so I can see the view?"

The tremors recurred several times. Then the area stabilized and became quiet. Inside my head, Domingo asked, "You like that Lieutenant Paisley a lot, don't you?"

"It's not any of your business."

"Everything's my business. Hey—" He stopped, then went on in a different voice, "Hey, what's going on?"

Total silence, just as if someone had clapped a hand over

152

Domingo's nonexistant mouth. I began to retrace my steps, down to the forest and bog. My head felt as if it were being divided into separate pieces. I could hardly think.

"Roxy!" Domingo almost split my brain in two.

"Trouble?"

"Upstairs. There's a fight in the hall. I can hear them."

"Call somebody."

"I can't call anybody but you. I'm not linked to anybody but you. If Dr. Mensy isn't with me, even she can't hear me."

"Okay, hold on. I'm coming in."

I tore into the forest at top speed, but as soon as I hit that wet, densely overgrown forest floor I had to slow down. The bogshoes over my shoulder caught on branches. I yanked them loose. Perhaps Dust Bowlers were heading into town; there must be people who saw them coming. I couldn't imagine a pitched battle in Bluebeard's Castle. We didn't have such things at home. But I wasn't at home, I was on a raw Jurassic-stage planet in a comparatively primitive society. I'd had nothing but surprises since I arrived, so I'd better be ready for a few more.

One of my feet caught in a clump of creepers and I sprawled hard on the ground. I rose up spitting, saw the glint of Cyclops as he fell and vanished, but couldn't stop to retrieve him.

Clumsy clod, I said to myself.

Hanging onto the bogshoes for dear life, I booted and batted my way through the steamy undergrowth toward the bog. Before I reached it, something stood in my way. It was about twenty feet tall at the head. Its jaws were peacefully chomping some thin, long leaves from a certain kind of tree.

It must have heard or smelled me because it turned its head, and the little glittering eyes looked me through and through. I stopped breathing. I became as invisible as possible. Domingo kept saying: "Hurry up, hurry up, they're coming to get me." But I didn't dare blink an eyelid.

After a few moments the reptile began to feed again, slowly chomping on the leaves, a few shreds and fibers dribbling down from its mouth. I felt sure the people in town could handle any trouble, but that did nothing to lessen my determination to get back there and help.

The reptile began to plod toward me, evidently looking for more of his special food. I went backwards, a step at a time, not sure of what I was stepping into. I ducked sideways and began to creep off a different way, figuring I could enter and cross the bog from another direction.

With a tremendous trampling rush, it came toward me, knocked me flat, and kept going. My back, my neck, my knees were bruised, though nothing seemed to be broken.

When I tried to get up, I fell over. I lay there for a while collecting myself. Next try I made it to my knees. Just bruises. Flailing around, hunting for the bogshoes, I spent a lot of time getting nowhere. Then I hobbled and hopped the rest of the way down to the bog, strapped on the shoes, and started across. I fell twice on the way. The second time it took me so long to get myself upright I nearly was pulled under. There was no message from Domingo, nothing. Hours had gone by. The link was wearing thin; perhaps it had gone completely and he was trying to speak to me but I couldn't hear.

Before I reached the edge of the forest I smelled smoke, a dirty, chemical smell as if all kinds of things were burning. Some Academy we're going to have, I thought furiously, crashing through toward the thin edge of the trees. Can't even control a small group, how are we going to teach them to control themselves? And how could anything in this place burn? But then I remembered that most of the houses were made of fanwood. It never rotted; it dried rapidly after being wet. Bluebeard's Castle, like the other buildings, was constructed mainly of fanwood.

There was a battle in the streets. Many houses were giving off a dirty brown smoke; people sat holding bloody heads or crawled around on their hands and knees looking for friends. To me, Dust Bowlers were indistinguishable from other Vogl people. Many people stood on the sidelines, staring at the melee, unwilling or unable to join in. They seemed to be in shock.

At the side entrance to Bluebeard's I knocked down a couple of people and thrust a few others aside. The minute I entered the building I began to cough and choke, though quenchers were being sprayed on the smoking walls. The air was vile. I headed for Dr. Mensy's office but the hall was full of people screaming, hitting each other, and stamping on those who had fallen.

Where was that damn door?

There was no answer, not in my head or aloud. I had to find a door myself and hope it was the right one. I went down the dark stairs, holding onto the grabrails, across a slippery, smoky area, to Domingo's room. The lights were on. The video screen and the speakers were smashed, wires hung loose, smoke dribbled up from one end of the computer. Panels had been torn off, bent, smashed. It was hard to believe so much damage could have been done.

I rolled the padded chair over, wondering if I could hook myself in and if there was anyone left to link to. But people had followed me down the stairs and now they burst into the room shouting and fighting. I was flattened against the wall, unable to move; the chair was knocked over.

Then a couple of Vogl Councilmen and a doctor with a shredded and bloody tunic came in the door and fired gas guns into the room. People toppled over in waves. My head caught fire, then my lungs. My nose turned into a pillow and I passed out.

155

◆

"Rimidon! Come on, Rimidon. On your feet!" A voice repeated this over and over as I came up through layers of unconsciousness. My eyes burned and my nose was filled with the smell of gas. Rike was leaning over me, calling me back to work. I reached out and tried to push him away.

"Come on, Officer," he repeated. "Up and at 'em."

"Nobody left," I mumbled.

"Sure, plenty left. Got to start school tomorrow."

I got my eyes open. Rike's long face hung in the air like a gloomy planet above me. "Hotel room?" I asked.

"Yeah, you been out awhile. We hauled you up here to give you some rest."

"What about Domingo?"

"I don't know."

"Everything under control?"

"You bet," Rike said. "They're just glueing the busted heads together now. The hospital's full up. Are you hungry?"

"No. I wish I were, I'd feel better."

"Oh, you're okay," Rike said. He sat on the edge of the bed and pushed the hair back from my face. "You're just a little bruised," he said. "Lovely shades of violet and purple."

"I fell. They're not even battle bruises."

"Sure they are. You want a citation or something? The sun must have gotten you." He stood up and patted my arm. "Stay in bed for a while. I'll see you later on."

I lay there, thinking confused thoughts about Vogl—the farm communities, the Dust Bowl chanters, and the incredibly sophisticated cyborgs. As Reba had said, at home we were working on a thousand different things, but here they'd concentrated on medical research. And maybe they'd done it not just because they could use this particular item, but because it

156

meant they had something to show us, something besides reems and beans, something we would want. It made sense.

How's Domingo? I asked the air, but the air didn't answer.

After a while I washed my face, put my cap on straight, and limped downstairs to the lobby. It was full of people talking and having drinks. Some of them were bandaged, lots of them were more bruised and shaken than I. Rike and Ben were over in a corner of the lounge. They called to me and I went to them and said, "I want to go right over to Dr. Mensy, I want to know what's happened over there."

Rike pulled me down onto the seat beside him. "Wait a moment, Roxy. I don't even know if you can get into that building."

"Sort of a direct hit, was it?" I asked.

Ben and Rike exchanged glances.

"Domingo's dead, isn't he? What was left of him, I mean."

"Well, they went straight for him," Rike said.

My eyes stung and I scrubbed tnem with my knuckles. "Damn gas guns," I said.

"Gas guns, nothing," Rike said, putting an arm around me.

We spent a few minutes in reflective silence. Reba pushed her way toward us through the chattering crowd. Her face was smudged with soot and there was a gash across one cheek-bone. A ragged bandage was wrapped around her left wrist. "Well," she said, as she plopped down next to Ben. "Bet you never expected a little exercise like that one."

"Is that what you call it?" I asked.

"Just a small local problem."

"Is there any good news?"

Reba smiled at me. "Sure there is. We never let them touch the Academy building. It's in fine shape. We can start classes there tomorrow."

"What about the Castle?" Ben asked.

157

"It's a shambles. Dr. Mensy's running around like crazy trying to patch it up, crying over Domingo, and giving orders three at a time." She glanced at me, then away. "One of the cydogs was broken to pieces but the other's okay. It keeps patrolling the corridor and everybody falls over it. It anesthetized Dr. Petes by mistake."

"I'm glad you find something amusing in the day's action," I said. "I even lost Cyclops."

"The last time they burned the whole town."

The three of us turned on her. "And you never said anything about that?" we demanded.

"I wouldn't want you to come up here with any preconceptions. The town's been burned over at least three times by various factions. Why do you think we've been demanding a Planet Patrol of our own?"

Rike stood up and took my hand. "Come on, Roxy," he said. "Let's get out and see what's happening in the town."

"Wait a minute, Rike," I said, hanging back.

"Now what?"

"I'm starving!"

Rike groaned, Reba laughed, and Captain Slane said mildly, "I believe the hotel dining room's still open."

"Try the bog custard," Reba suggested as we walked off toward the dining room.

"Is there really such a thing?" I asked Rike as we sat down. "Bog custard?"

"Well, I don't know for sure. Yes, here it is." He pointed it out on the menu. "I'll have one, too, for dessert. After we eat we can try to get in touch with Dr. Mensy."

I shook my head. "No, I'd rather not just now." When I looked up, Rike was paying very close attention to my face. His brow was wrinkled with worry. "I'm all right," I said to reassure him. "But I lost Domingo."

Rike snorted with anger. "That's ridiculous," he said. "You

did everything you could, you couldn't possibly have come back in time to save him, nor could you possibly have held out against twenty or thirty people in that room. I don't want to hear that from you again." The wrinkles vanished from his brow and he smiled a little. "You just feel terrible that he's gone. You can say it. It's all right, you know."

"Yes, I know. But in the end, there isn't any way of saying it, Rike. Thanks, though."

"Then stop off at the Castle in the morning, first thing. I think it'll make you feel better."

◆

I woke up in the morning remembering what he'd said and decided he was right. Except I swore I'd start calling that building Medical Research from now on and never again refer to it as Bluebeard's Castle.

The halls were full of wreckage and workmen who were starting to clear it away. Dr. Petes came out of a room, his arms full of empty fire-quencher cans. I called to him, "Is Dr. Mensy here?"

"Busy," he said. He was going off, but I ran after him.

"I have to talk to her."

"Not this morning, Officer," he said. "She was up all night and this morning she's working."

Just then the door at the top of the stairway opened and Dr. Mensy looked out, saying, "Dr. Petes? Has that body been disposed of yet?" Then she saw me. "Oh, hello, sweetheart," she said, red-eyed and intense. "We lost the boy."

"I know. I came by to say how sorry I am."

"Not half as sorry as we are. But we salvaged a lot of the bionic system and we have a new—" She broke off as an orderly came down the corridor wheeling a cart. My first thought was that he was bringing dinner. There was a metal tray on the cart.

Covering the tray was one of those big metal helmets they use in fancy restaurants to keep the food warm, but this cover had icy moisture condensed on it and it was rimmed with refrigerant pipe.

"Alas, poor Dust Bowler," Dr. Petes said.

"Don't start with sarcasm," Annie Mensy warned him. "We'll have enough trouble trying to seal it into a place and bring her to without you reminding her of what she was."

They had forgotten me, so after I'd seen them slide the cart onto a pair of tracks going down the stairway to what used to be Domingo's room, I turned and went back. The roof of the building gaped open in several places, letting the cooled air out and the hot, steamy air in. I hoped the downstairs room was tight. If not the engineers would stifle before they got that brain connected. The cydog was now resting under some shrubs outside.

"You're late," Capt. Ben Slane said when I arrived. "Your first class is waiting. Third door to the right. And good luck, Officer." He had already picked up and assimilated that Vogl expression of blankness which I detested.

Third door to the right, maybe half a dozen students waiting to see me show off my stuff—if I could remember a single thing. I opened the door. They were sitting in chairs, lounging on the floor, leaning against the walls, more than twenty of them. All shapes, sizes, colors, all wearing that "I don't know you" look.

Somebody had taken away the chair I was supposed to use so I slid up on the table, sitting there and wishing I could trade my boots for bare feet. The cooling system wasn't in operation yet.

"Today," I said, "we're going to learn how to handle mobs."

My mob broke into approving grins.

The class went well. They were all eager to learn. If they didn't treat me like a teacher it was only because they regarded me as some kind of impersonal resource from which they could

160

pick out the knowledge they needed. After being taken aback by the lack of respect, I decided it was a very good thing. After all, I was here only to give them all I knew that could help them. And this was a frontier society, where first things came first, and no time was wasted.

No one hung around after class was over. I was on my way out, past Captain Slane's office, when he called me in. Rike was there, too, looking pleased about something.

"There's some news," Ben Slane said. "Why don't you sit down for a minute?"

I tried the Vogl slump on one of those awful chairs, figuring it was time I learned how to do it and look natural.

Ben said, "Corporal Doucette's taking the next freighter up and bringing back your shoulder patch, according to the message."

"My what?" I exclaimed, amazed.

"You've got rank," Captain Slane said. "You've made corporal. The Patrol does reward its hard-working members, you know, and that was no easy job you took on, being linked to a cyborg."

I was speechless. Linked I may have been, and hard-working certainly, but I hadn't been able to save Domingo and felt like a total failure.

As usual, Rike knew what I was thinking. He came over and put his hand on my shoulder. "Come on, Corporal," he said. "I discovered the hotel has a swimming pool. How about it?"

"You're dismissed," Ben Slane said just to remind us who he was. But as I got to my feet I saw him suddenly turn toward Rike and wink.

Designed by Leslie Bauman
The text type is 11/14 Primer and the display is Cornered